THE SCHOOLMASTER

Earl Lovelace is a novelist, playwright and essayist who lives and works in Trinidad and Tobago. Among many honours and positions, he was the Distinguished Novelist in the Department of English at the Pacific Lutheran University, Tacoma, Washington (1999–2005), and his schooling includes the Eastern Caribbean Institute of Agriculture and Forestry, Howard University and Johns Hopkins University, from which he holds the Master of Arts degree. His novels include *Salt*, which won the 1997 Commonwealth Writers' Prize, *The Wine of Astonishment* (1982), *The Dragon Can't Dance* (1979), *The Schoolmaster* (1968) and *While Gods Are Falling* (1965), winner of the British Petroleum Independence Literary Award. His short stories appear in the collection *A Brief Conversion and Other Stories* (1988); his selected essays appear in *Growing in the Dark* (2003); and a film of his story 'Joebell and America', with a screenplay co-authored with his daughter Asha, was produced in September 2004.

by the same author

fiction
WHILE GODS ARE FALLING
THE DRAGON CAN'T DANCE
THE WINE OF ASTONISHMENT
A BRIEF CONVERSION AND OTHER STORIES
SALT
IS JUST A MOVIE

plays
JESTINA'S CALYPSO

EARL LOVELACE

THE SCHOOLMASTER

faber

First published by Collins in 1968

This paperback edition first published in 2024
by Faber & Faber Ltd
The Bindery, 51 Hatton Garden
London EC1N 8HN

Printed and bound by CPI Group (UK) Ltd, Croydon, CR0 4YY

A CIP record for this book
is available from the British Library

ISBN 978–0–571–19676–0

6 8 10 9 7 5

Part One

Chapter One

I

Dry season reach now. Sunlight blazes the hills; and scattered between the hills' valuable timber trees – the cedar, angelin, laurier-matack, galba and mahoe – the poui is dropping rich yellow flowers like a madman throwing away gold. Down on the flat and in the crotches of the land where the two rivers stagger through the blue stone so plentiful in Kumaca, the water is clear, and in places, ice cold. The soil is rich, deep and black. The immortelle holds its scarlet blossoms still, and on the stems of cocoa, which it shades, pods have turned yellow or red and are waiting. It is time. The cocoa is ready for harvesting.

In the village the harvest is something to think of. It brings money into the humblest household; and even to a people whose needs are simple, desires few, whose women burn dried wood in firesides made of clay, money is a great something. For there is the account at the shop of Dardain that one needs to pay; and one has his eyes on a radio such as the one that Consantine Patron plays in his house; and maybe among the men there are those who would like to leave Kumaca for a few days and go down to the plain beyond the hill and the forest and the broken balata bridge where in the wet season and even in the dry landslides fill the track with loose earth and mud, and one must get off the donkeys and go on foot – go down – past Valencia to the town of Zanilla with the big court-house building and the tall policemen and many radios playing in the shops of the clean streets and the green painted cinema house where for a price you can go in and watch men on horses shoot guns off and make fine talk and kiss pretty girls, and where in the crowded rumshops it is easy to get drunk again with friends of the year before.

And there are those among the young men who are itching to travel to that big, fast and terrible city that is Port-of-Spain to watch tramcars run on rails of steel in the streets of asphalt and to look at the big signs which they wish they could read. But this is a dream, for very few of the villagers in their lives have been to the city, except

7

Consantine Patron, Paulaine Dandrade and Dardain the shopkeeper, who actually worked in the city for some time.

But above every other thought what is uppermost in the minds of all Kumaca is that big fête at the end of the harvest when Easter is beginning. People come from Valencia, from Zanilla, even from Mamoral and as far as Blanchisseuse. That is *fête papa!* with such eating: wild meats caught by the men and prepared by the women, and farine from cassava, and corn-and-sweet-potato paimee; and drinking rum, fruit wines from cashew and guava, and sorrel and mauby; and singing and dancing. There is the orchestra led by Miguel, the white-haired brother of Consantine Patron, with the fiddle and the quatros and flute and tambourines of Sension and Martin and Felix Paponette. Then the sports with running races and climbing the greasy pole and the tug-of-war which brings always so much laughter, and the eating competition which is so often won by Landeau who is also the champion stickfighter. And there are the cockfights which are in themselves another festival, with cocks coming all the way from Diego Martin and Maraval. This the villagers think of; but first, they work.

The cocoa pods must be picked with the knife-sharp goulets on the ends of long, slim bamboo rods, gathered, opened, the beans taken out by the women and put in baskets to be taken to the fermentary where they must remain for at least one week before being removed and spread in the sun to dry; and even then that is not the end, because the time comes when the beans must be polished by the men and women dancing upon them with their bare feet with much singing and clapping of hands; then only are the beans bagged and taken to the shop of Dardain who has a licence from the government to deal in cocoa.

Yes, it is much work. This was what young Pedro Assivero, labouring on the estate of Paulaine Dandrade, was thinking as he carried the basketful of wet beans upon his head from the field to the donkey cart on the track across the drain. Work! Work and Pedro were no great friends. Mischief and music: yes; work no. But how else could he get money to buy the fawn-coloured tweed pants and the long-sleeved blue shirt that he had seen at the shop of Dardain? Christiana, the daughter of Mr Paulaine, would be at the fête and he would want to ask her to dance, and he would want to play again for her on the flute he had made with his own hands from the thin bamboo that grows at the edge of the river, and sing for her a song, and maybe say to her face the soft words of his heart that were so hard to speak. Work, yes.

Pedro came out of the field, crossed the drain and reached the track where the donkey in harness was cropping grass and with its long ears flicking flies off its face. It was past midday, but in the shade it was cool. Miguel Paponette, a square-faced, quarrelsome-looking man, tanned and furrowed like the wrong side of old leather, was sitting on a wood stump with one eye closed, peacefully smoking his pipe. His job was to tend the donkey cart. When it became full of beans, he would take it up to the fermentary in the yard. Pedro looked at old Miguel sitting there with the trees hushing around him, the smoke lifting in a lazy stir from his pipe, and he thought: Old man, you are too comfortable, yes. His eyes shone with mischief and a smile cracked his broad, flat face, stretched his wide mouth. For now he was thinking how best he could alarm old Miguel, take him from his lazy comfort and peace.

Innocently, he walked up to the cart, leaned the basket on his head, and let the beans fall into the tray of the cart. He smiled again, secretly, barely showing it on his face. He was thinking to tease Miguel about his gamecocks. In the old days, Miguel had owned some good cocks that had won many battles both in Valencia and at Kumaca, but now, although he loved the cockfights as passionately, his cocks were badly trained, and too slow, and the battles they won were few and far between. Still, Miguel would not give up. He felt that he had the best cocks in Kumaca, and that he was only unlucky. Now at the cockfights, he would squat at the very edge of the gayelle, and look at his birds being raked with spurs, and tears would come into his eyes, and he would talk about the one great gamecock that he owned, a black called Hawk who was a great killer and about whom he claimed there was no greater. And it was only by this talking about Hawk that he seemed to manage to bear the failure of his current breed of cocks.

Pedro took up the empty basket, turned and began to walk towards Miguel. He was not smiling now. Suddenly, with a very dramatic movement, he froze.

'Snake! Miguel!' he shouted in an urgent whisper. 'Cousin Miguel! Do not move! Behind you! A snake! Mappipire!'

The old one opened his other eye, became alert.

'No!' Pedro pleaded. 'Do not turn! Quiet! Wait! It is walking away. Wait!'

Miguel's body tensed, and he held the pipe firmly between his teeth His eyes were looking at Pedro. Pedro waited, frozen. Then he breathed a huge sigh of relief.

'You can get up now. It is gone.'

Miguel did not jump. He turned and looked behind him.

'Where is the snake?'

'Gone now. It was right behind you. You were lucky. I have not seen, ever, such a huge size of mappipire. Do you walk with old Spanish prayers to protect yourself?'

'But how come I do not hear it?' Miguel asked suspiciously.

He got up now.

'Do not play a game with me, boy.'

'But you did not hear the leaves shake behind your back?' Pedro asked.

'Maybe I hear the leaves shake, and maybe I don't hear the leaves shake. But I do not think there was a snake behind me. You know I do not play a game with like your size,' Miguel said.

Pedro kept his face very serious. He shrugged.

'Well, there was a snake behind you. I swear. Right behind you. A big-big snake.' Pedro opened his arms to show the hugeness of the snake.

'I do not believe you,' Miguel said.

In his mind Pedro thought: Ah, that was good. But not so good. I will have to tease him a little about his cocks, then I will laugh. Pedro shuffled his bare feet on the ground.

'Well, Cousin Miguel, soon the season is here. You putting down any cocks in the gayelle?'

Miguel returned to his seat on the wood stump. He took out his tobacco and was putting some in his pipe. He looked up.

'If I do not put down my cocks, there is no battle in Kumaca. You know that.'

'But I hear . . .' Pedro said. 'I hear things about your cocks. You do not hear what they say?'

'What they say? What can they say? Is years now I have the best cocks in Kumaca. This time I will not be unlucky. What they say, eh?'

10

Pedro shifted nervously. Then made a step in Miguel's direction.

'I do not think it is fair what they way. They say that your cocks are like fowls for the table. They say they are not even good *cariadols* for the real fighters to spar with.'

Miguel jumped to his feet.

'They say that! Those jackass say that! I who have the best gamecocks from here to Maraval, and win twenty-nine battles with Hawk alone before they poison him near the gayelle in Valencia when we went to fight. And I couldn't even get them to pit their cock with Hawk. Those jackass say that! And none in Kumaca could stand up with Hawk.'

'But Hawk dead, Cousin Miguel.'

Miguel said sadly, 'Yes, Hawk is dead. But I will bring again in the gayelle a cock like Hawk, this very Easter. Those jackass! I will show them cock!'

'And they say, Cousin, that you cry too much at the gayelle, when the spurs of the gamecocks sink into the necks of your *cariadols*.'

'Who say that? Who say that?' Miguel asked hotly, growing angry, and moving up and down like a stickfighter in a rage.

Pedro gave a vague jerk of his head.

'They ... But you must not worry too much if your cocks are *cariadols*, for you can always put them in the pot. And if you have not the heart to do it, then give them to me. And if you cry a little in the gayelle? What means a few drops of water from your eyes? Eh, Cousin?' Pedro said very sympathetically.

'You!' Miguel cried, stammering with rage. 'You ... Do not call me cousin. I am not cousin to you.'

'But, Cousin Miguel – '

'So you say that my cocks are – '

Miguel reached for the nearest weapon at hand – a piece of wood – and flung it at Pedro, who dodged it happily, and backed off into the field, slowly enough to encourage Miguel to reach for more missiles to fly at him, and to stream upon him accompanying showers of abuse in a voice tight with anger and frustration. Then was young Pedro satisfied.

Back in the field, Pedro found as he had hoped and half expected that the work for the day was just ending. The women were opening

11

the last few pods of cocoa, and the pickers removing the goulet-knives from the ends of bamboo rods. Mr Paulaine, his khaki shirt stained with perspiration, his poniard-case swinging at his side, his broad face glistening with sunlight and perspiration, was moving among the workers, making a joke with the women, offering cigarettes to the men, and looking to see that all baskets and implements were collected, and everything was in order before the return to the yard. Pedro set himself briskly to doing nothing, then when all was ready, he turned the cocoa basket upside down on his head, so that it looked like a gigantic hat, took his flute from his back pocket, and began to play the tune to a work-song that was popular in Kumaca. Then the singing began; one man first, then two; then the entire body of workers were singing along the track towards the yard. The song grew, the song swelled, the voices of the women reached high, and the voices of the men rumbled in the background like a thunder that is distant, that you can hardly hear when the rain is not too far off, and clouds have wings spread across the sky, and trees shiver like pups left outdoors on the steps when it's raining.

In the yard now the singing died away, the workers went to put up the baskets and implements. Pedro looked at the house of Paulaine Dandrade, and struck his flute against the edge of his palm to clear out the spittle that might have gathered in it, then he put the flute in his back pocket, carried the empty basket to add to the pile kept in a section of the cocoa house. He kept looking at the house, but he did not see her. He saw three of her five brothers, but Christiana he did not see, and it was time to leave. All the workers were leaving. He did not want to leave without sight of her face, but he could not remain in the place of Paulaine Dandrade for ever. It was no use. He would have to leave. He continued to look at the house as he walked away very, very slowly, then he took out his flute, fitted it to his lips. He had different tunes to play her; and now that sadness was on him like rain, and he longed so to see her face, he played a soft, wailing tune, full of sweet, sad notes, that was like the cry of a young animal that was lost and knew not where to turn.

Pedro took the track through the estate of Mr Paulaine, cut through the estate of Carrera, then through the estate of Consantine Patron, which is the largest estate in Kumaca and stretched up the hills to the forest where the wild beasts and the monkeys make their home; and all the time he played his wailing notes. He stopped playing only when he came to the track that led to the back of the little wooden house in which he lived with his mother, father, and younger brother. He had three other brothers and three sisters but they had all left home to set up homes for themselves.

His brother, Robert, the boy after him, was there at the back of the house, splitting firewood with an axe. He stopped cutting the wood and watched Pedro come up. He was glad to see his brother.

'You work late today, eh, Pedro.'

'It is the last day. We finish the picking. Did Papa say when we begin to pick the little on our place?' Pedro asked.

'He did not say. Perhaps tonight when he comes he say.'

'If he is not too drunk. For me, we can start to pick it tomorrow,' Pedro said.

'Why he drinks so much Pedro?'

Pedro picked up a piece of the split wood, and beat a rhythm with it on the side of his leg.

'Boy, maybe it is because he remembers how much he lost gambling on the cocks, and how we have hardly any land left. And he looks at Mama, and Mama knows, and she looks at him, and he feels it because she makes no complain. And there was a time, Mama says, he would go to Valencia at the head of the team of cockfighters, and he was very brave, and they say he bet too heavy, and first he was very lucky, but then he was not lucky, and he would not stop. He would bet heavy, and he would lose. He was something like Miguel who I play a joke on today. But our father, he is maybe worse, because Miguel never had children.'

'It is bad with Papa, Pedro.'

'Yes. Now he picks cocoa on the estate of Consantine Patron, and dies daily inside himself, because Mama is looking at him and does not complain, and because he knows the man he was, and remembers, and goes again and again to the shop of Dardain.'

'Too often he goes, Pedro.'

'Maybe one day he does not go any more. Where is he now. You know?'

'He is at the place of Consantine Patron.'

'Consantine Patron, you say. They not finish with the picking over there yet?'

'They will finish today or tomorrow.'

'I am hungry,' Pedro said, turning to go.

Robert slid one hand along the smooth wood of the axe-handle.

'Pedro, what is the talk about the school now?'

'I hear they will talk again this evening at the place of Dardain.'

'You think they will really have a school in Kumaca? I will like for a school to come. I will learn to read. I will read the best in the village, and only you will learn to read better than me. Eh, Pedro? You think we will have a school here, brother?'

'I think yes, we will have the school. But I do not know when. They talk about it for six months. Today they agree, tomorrow they do not agree. But Mr Paulaine keeps on talking about this school, and now even Dardain agrees that it is a good thing.'

'I hear that Christiana, the daughter of Mr Paulaine, is very good at the reading. I will like to go to school, Pedro.'

'It is good for you. You will learn to read and write for both of us. I am too old for school now. I am a man.'

Robert said, 'But they say, Pedro, that the school will be for big and little, that even our Papa can learn in the school.'

'Papa will not go into the school. And do not ever forget and make that talk with him.'

'But I do not understand. Mr Paulaine can read, and Consantine Patron can read, why our father will not go to the school?'

'He will not go. It is his pride. He is not a child.'

'And you, Pedro? In serious?'

'Me? Boy, I know to hunt in the forest of Kumaca, and I know by the scratch on the ground, if it is a lappe or 'gouti. I know when the cocoa is to pick, and when it is to prune, and how long it must remain in the fermentary, and how long to dry in the sun, and I can count the money that Dardain gives for the crop.

'And, Robert, I have made with my own hands a flute from the thin bamboo that grows at the edge of the river, and I can play, and can sing. But I tell you, Robert, it will be a fine thing. And I will like to know to read and to write. So then I can write a letter to Christiana, and she can read it. And if she will write me a letter, I cannot carry

14

such a letter to ask Mr Paulaine who is her father to read it for me, and I would not like to carry it to Dardain and I do not much care to take it to Consantine Patron who would maybe laugh. But in truth, I am ashamed to be sitting learning A B C with all the little children of the village.'

'Big men will be learning too. And look at me,' Robert said.

'You have only thirteen years. I will be glad if the men will go to the school, then I will not feel so bad.'

'But it is a good thing, eh, Pedro. Mr Paulaine says it is a good thing.'

'And Consantine Patron remains quiet. He does not often agree with Mr Paulaine. But that is because they are two big men.'

'Which one you think is more bigger, Pedro?'

'In some things it is Consantine Patron. And by the way he walks and his talk say he is a big man to his throat. But the people like Mr Paulaine, and that makes him very big, and perhaps in his heart he is bigger than Consantine Patron. But you never can tell with Consantine.'

'I hope our Papa goes to the meeting to tell us what happens,' Robert said.

'He will go,' Pedro said.

'I hope we get the school.'

'Yes, Robert. It will be a very wonderful thing to write a letter to Christiana.'

II

Consantine Patron could read. He carried in one of the pockets of his shirt a pair of reading glasses which he had bought from the eye doctor at Zanilla, and, clipped to the other pocket, two fountain pens. He was the last to arrive at the shop of Dardain where on the suggestion of Paulaine Dandrade the men of the village had gathered to talk about the building of a school in Kumaca. Consantine Patron sat on the chair left for him between old Lucein, his father-in-law, and Dardain. He crossed his legs and kept his lean, brown face very serious, very severe, and (he imagined) very learned, for that was his style. He was not given to much laughing and joking in public, and at the cockfights, even when his cocks won their battles there was a look on his face that was a smile and yet not a smile; and there was something that made his laugh not a real laugh.

Now that he had arrived, the men knew that the talking would begin soon. They were correct. Patron glanced at Dardain and Dardain looked at old Lucien, the father of Consantine Patron's wife, and Lucien nodded. Lucien was now a very old man, one of the oldest in Kumaca, and because of the property he owned (which would all pass to Consantine Patron now, because Lucien had no other child but the daughter who was Patron's wife) and because of the weight of his position, and his name and the respect that these and his personal actions in Kumaca had gained for him during the years, he was, despite his age, still considered the man in the village, and at a meeting like this one would be the one privileged to speak first.

He had been smoking his pipe, and now he placed it on the table before him. He lifted his head and with his old yellowed eyes looked around slowly and saw that the faces of the men were turned to him, and that they were waiting for his words.

'The talk we have to make this evening is about building a school in Kumaca,' old Lucien said, speaking very slowly as if he were listening to every single word before he ventured to utter the other following it.

'But I am an old man.'

He said this as if he had been thinking of it for a long time over and over again and didn't really, really couldn't believe it, and there was a far sadness in his voice and he nodded his head slowly.

'An old man who in his day sip his coffee when it is hot, and all his life drink the waters of Kumaca. My hair is white now, voices are calling in my head. My eyes hear talk and my eyes see dimly like an old man's eyes. You say you want a school to come in Kumaca. I listen to you. I look at your face and see not many lines. I watch how you walk and how you sit down and how you get up, and I watch how you work in the cocoa and I know that you are not like me who to walk must put one foot first then draw up the other behind it. And now when my coffee is hot I sip it. But I am an old man that you allow to speak because of his age and out of his time . . . But I say this now! Your tomorrow I will not see, and maybe your school. I have

16

never been to school and I have finished school. So let me first listen to the ones whose hair is not white as mine, for it is your matter, and with my age now let me first wait and listen.'

Consantine Patron looked at his father-in-law and he thought: Soon we must make ready a coffin for this old man. Death has his spurs close to his neck. His words have too many leaves and too few branches.

Old Lucien took up his pipe and fumbled in the pocket of his trousers for matches, then he remembered that he was directing the proceedings. He turned and looked at Paulaine Dandrade who was sitting next to him, and while Paulaine got to his feet, Lucien lit the pipe with trembling fingers, then took three quick puffs so that the lighted tobacco glowed in the bowl of the pipe and the smoke rose tiredly and white above his white hair.

Yes, Consantine Patron thought, he is very old. We must be ready soon for a wake. Now let us hear what this good Paulaine says.

Paulaine was saying

'How long again do we talk about this school before we make some action? In the time of my childhood there was no school in Kumaca, but a lady gave lessons to a few of us. It is how many years I was a child? Today all about in this country people are learning to read and write, but in Kumaca we do not have a school. Our children do not learn to read and write. We remain backward in this place. The world is moving forward. Like a fist the world is closing around Kumaca, and soon maybe we are the only people whose children cannot spell their names. Go to the village of Valencia that is only eleven miles away and you will see the changes taking place there. Go to Zanilla! And Armia that was so much high woods just some years ago now have big buildings going up, and it is something to hear the people talk about what is written in the newspapers. What is wrong with Kumaca? I do not say we live very bad here. Yes, we hunt in the forest. We catch fish in the rivers, and have our fêtes and cockfights. But we live just as our fathers live. But they are dead and their time gone. We have to go forward. A school for Kumaca is too much? Tell me! Our children will go to Port-of-Spain, they will not know how to read the picture poster or the sign which tells the name of the street. That is not good. Eh, tell me, is that good for the children of Kumaca?'

17

Consantine Patron watched and felt how the softness stole among the men as Paulaine spoke; and because he felt the tug of softness too, he forced a further stiffness into his features. Consantine Patron loved Kumaca too.

Paulaine was saying:

'What is to frighten us in this matter? Nothing! I say let us approach the priest at Zanilla and let him tell us what we should do to get a school. But also let us prepare to do the work for ourselves now. We are not rich here, but we have strength to work, eh?' And we have a forest fill-up with good timber. No. It is not nice, I tell you, when a man here looks at the newspaper and cannot read it, and cannot read the names on the deeds of his own lands; and what about writing a letter? We must think about these things because we are living here now, and for our children we must care too. Eh, is that too much for Kumaca?'

Paulaine Dandrade sat down and the eyes turned now upon Consantine Patron, because everyone expected him not only to speak, but to oppose what Paulaine had put forward. It was the familiar pattern. In a cockfight, if Paulaine put a cock in the gayelle, Consantine Patron put one in to match it. And if Paulaine said corn, Consantine Patron was almost certain to say peas. This had been so far back to their boyhood. And sometimes Consantine Patron came out the better, and sometimes Paulaine did.

Consantine Patron with his severe face, his hawk nose almost touching his moustached lip, thought: Wait!

He knew the men and what they were expecting from him, but this was a serious matter.

But now Dardain, the shopkeeper, was on his feet. He was a small nervous man with greying hair, a thin, pale face, a way of speaking a little too loudly as if he was himself deaf, and a terrible habit of pointing his right index finger in the face of whomsoever he was speaking to. With much gesticulating Dardain was saying.

'Paulaine talk words with sense. I say, let us build a school. Let us have the good books to educate the people in the right and proper way.'

Consantine Patron thought: Why have you changed your tune so suddenly, old mongoose? Ah! With the building of the school you will supply some of the materials, and you will sell the books in your shop. Ah! But maybe you are not so smart, eh? Will you sell as much

18

rum as before? And will the people want you to write their letters for them when they learn how to do it themselves? What do you have up your sleeves, Mr Mongoose?

Dardain was saying:

'I do not think of myself in this matter. I think of Kumaca. And I know it is better for you to learn for yourself than if I or anyone should read or write for you. Paulaine say good words with much sense.'

And turning now to look at Consantine Patron, Dardain said: 'And there are many more good words to follow.'

He sat down. He had spoken rather quickly, in very much the same manner as a fast eater attempting to devour a plate of hot food.

The eyes looked now at Consantine Patron who was already in the act of standing.

Consantine was thinking that if the school came to Kumaca there would be little respect for his own ability as a man of letters, and that anybody would, when he learned to read a little, be able to sit down on the bench in front of the shop of Dardain and read the newspapers, and would feel himself entitled to wear fountain pens in his pockets, and some even would strain their pockets to buy reading glasses from the eye doctor in Zanilla. And what would become of the cocoa when the young men must go to school? And what will happen when they all want to go now to the city of Port-of-Spain, or to the town of Zanilla, because they could read what is written on the signboards? And he was thinking that the men had listened well to Paulaine, and that soon Lucien would die, then it would be either Paulaine or himself who would take the place of honour in Kumaca, and would have the privilege of inviting the priest to his house, and would go to Valencia at the head of the team of cockfighters, and would say the prayers at the funerals when the priest was absent.

Yes, Paulaine had used his words well. And Dardain . . . He knew Dardain too well. If Dardain supported the building of the school it was certain that he had already worked out a means of making some big gain for himself out of it. But what it was he could not figure out. But now he must talk. The men were waiting.

Consantine Patron reached into his breast pocket for his eye glasses, held them in his hands, and was speaking.

'I do not say that a school is not a good thing. I say that Papa Lucien has many grey hairs yet hear what he says. He says that he sips his coffee when it is hot. I say that too. I say let us think carefully what we do. When everybody goes to school, who will pick the cocoa? Who will go for the wood to make the fire to cook the food that we must eat? And I ask, who will teach in the school? And where will we build the school? Who will pay for the building? Do we have the money to pay? And will we have to pay to learn in the school? Who will pay the schoolmaster?'

Consantine Patron put the spectacles on his face and fitted the handles behind his ears.

'And the teacher? Where will he live? Is he to come outside of Kumaca? And who in Kumaca knows how to teach? And if he is to come from outside, he cannot travel every day because of the bad road. What to do?

'It is very good to be able to read, and it is a wonderful thing to write a letter to the newspapers as you know I myself wrote the time of the big landslide when the road was blocked and we couldn't get through to Valencia and had to go through the big forest and out to the sea through Platanal to Toco. In my heart I think there is not greater thing than for a man to sign his name at the bottom of a letter whose words he has written with his own hands. But I say still that we must not forget to sip our coffee when it is hot, and to do those things which we can do.'

Consantine Patron sat down. He saw old Lucien nodding his head, saw Paulaine shift in his seat, look around as if he would speak. Dardain also looked like he wanted to get to his legs, but it was Lucien the dried old man who had the right, and it was he who first opened his mouth to speak in his slow, trembly, dragging tone with the edge of excitement pitching his voice to a higher key.

'I sip my coffee when it is hot. My hair is white like cured cedar and my tongue tough; if I take a swallow now it would not matter. A kitten does not drink hot milk.'

Lucien sat very still, his head slightly bent, his eyes closed, puffing his pipe, his whole face pulsing like the throat of an excited bull frog, his scraggy beard touching the collar of his once-white shirt.

Dardain was on his legs.

'Consantine Patron can read, and his reasoning is good. I agree with him. We must think carefully what we are doing. We cannot build a school in the air. We must have a teacher, and know where he will stay, and how we will pay him. That is why we gather here. But even Consantine knows that the young men will not spend all their time in the school or with the newspapers. It is for the good of all. We must build this school. But we must know what we are doing. The priest at Zanilla knows us and we know him. I say, let Consantine go with Paulaine and ask the questions and get the answers and listen to what the priest advise on the building of the school.'

'The priest is coming to Kumaca the week before Good Friday, we can speak to him then. After the mass would be a good time,' Consantine Patron said.

'That is too sorrowful a time to make such talk Lucien said. 'It is better to go to see him at Zanilla. Then he would know we mean business.'

There was much talk now, with the other men joining in and giving their views, supporting both the idea of the school and the suggestion that the priest be consulted. Only Miguel Paponette, the great trainer of fighting cocks, disagreed wholeheartedly. He had never been to school, he said, and didn't know how to read or to write. He had heard that much reading and writing made a man go out of his head, and saw no reason for this great concern about school. What should be done was that a road be built and more cocoa planted in Kumaca. He wasn't very convincing, principally because he himself did not seem to believe or to understand what he was saying; and his words caused much laughter. So it was decided that Consantine Patron and Paulaine Dandrade should go to Zanilla to see the priest.

'This is a very busy time of year for me,' Consantine Patron said. 'I do not want to leave Kumaca now, but I will tell my questions to Paulaine and he can ask the priest for the answers, and anyway, one man makes better talk than two, because he knows what is in his own head, and does not know what is in the head of the man with him.'

So it was agreed. Paulaine Dandrade would go to see the priest at Zanilla and make a plea for a school in Kumaca.

Chapter Two

I

Father Vincent did not often forget that he was a priest. But this morning (he had just come from the church where he had said his first mass for the day), standing at the white latticed window of the white-painted, low-roofed presbytery, looking past the parted, cream-coloured lace curtains with the frayed edges, which the cleaner never removed until he had told her to take them down half a dozen times at least, across the green lawn and orchard of mango trees blossoming white and humming with bees, past the row of young coconut palms with the gentle breeze and early sunshine lifting and lighting their leaves, to the manjack tree with the birds singing in its green branches, with open beaks and gurgling throats – how he was lost looking at the birds' throats! – he forgot, and listened and watched the birds sing then fly off in pairs, first one, then the other pursuing, getting alongside, above the trampled slope bare of grass now, past the now grave-quiet schoolyard, to the chenette tree standing in the little clearing above and on the edge of the town of Zanilla.

But now he heard the bell ring at the gate and knew, even before he turned to the sound with an instant return of sadness and guilt at having strayed, that he was not a man, came back from himself to his vows and priesthood into which he had entered perhaps since his quiet childhood and more finally that time when he returned from university and found early autumn stripping the trees and found nothing to make him want to change. Caroline who lived across the lake near which as children they had played was gone, married, and his brother, Wallis, had left to become a salesman with a firm in Dublin, and his father sat there in the house with his rheumatism, looking out his now dimmed eyes grumbling, 'The Irish will fight, The Irish will fight,' and nothing, nothing. Everything seemed so ordinary, so uninspiring, and his choice which was made since his childhood was confirmed that autumn. So he became a priest, believing that in that choice he could reduce the nothingness and lift the spirit of man;

and now his neck was tanned with sixteen years of sun, and the bell at the gate was ringing.

Father Vincent had been expecting the carpenters to come in to do some repairs on the church that morning, but as he turned and walked briskly to the door, he thought that it wasn't, couldn't possibly at this early hour be the carpenters. He was not wrong. The man at the gate was no carpenter. He was tall, slim, brown, about the priest's own age, with a rather flat, Spanish-looking face off which the moustaches had very recently been shaved. He wore a brown felt hat turned up at the brim, a pair of brown leather boots, and his white shirt, which still bore the wrinkles of its newness, was buttoned at the wrists and at the neck. Father Vincent did not forget a face.

'Good morning,' he said in his cheerful, aggressive manner, opening the gate, fixing the man with his fierce little blue eyes, and searching in his memory for the man's name.

'Good morning, Father-priest.'

'Ah! Yes. It is Kumaca. Mr Dandrade, how are you?'

'I am well, thank you, Father-priest. I come to talk with you. It is about the school that we need at Kumaca.'

'Come in and sit down. You have come very early.'

Paulaine Dandrade went through the door. He took off his hat, and sat on the very first chair he came to.

'Yes,' he said, 'I reached Valencia yesterday night, and I came from there at daybreak. I know you are so busy. I want to meet you, so I come early.'

'It was good to come at this time. I am expecting the carpenters in to repair our little church later this morning. Tell me about this school that you need.'

'We would like very much for a school to be built in Kumaca, Father-priest. There is no place for the children to learn to read and write. Many of the boys go away from Kumaca, and come even to Zanilla; they cannot write. They do not know to read. It is education that everyone needs today, and we by ourselves cannot give it to our children, so we decided, and I come from the village to speak to you, and to ask you to help us with a school. We are Catholics in Kumaca, and would like very much for a Catholic school.'

'Yes,' Father Vincent said, when Paulaine had finished. 'Yes. I will try to help you in whatever way I can. Have you ever had a school at Kumaca?'

'Except for a woman who in my childhood kept school in a little house, there is no school at Kumaca.'

'And you think you should have one now?'

'We think that, yes. In the old days, maybe it was not so important, but now a man who cannot write a letter and read the newspapers is nothing. Later it will be worse for him.'

'In the town of Zanilla,' Father Vincent said, 'there are many who read newspapers and write letters, and there are many, many more in the city. And the Church finds that there is more sin in Zanilla, and much more in the city where the people do so well with letters and newspapers. It is something to think of, Mr Dandrade.'

'I have seen the city, Father-priest. I agree it is not very nice.'

'It is terrible. And your people are simple, Mr Dandrade. Good people,' the priest said.

'And you think that for us to learn, it will not be good, Father-priest?'

'It is something to think of. Perhaps what you need, Mr Dandrade, is for someone to give lessons to a few who can profit by them. You do not need too many going to school. Your way of life is different ... I mean, you grow your cocoa, and hunt in the forest, and you have a way of life that is related to your economic and social situation. Perhaps what you might do is to find someone in your village to write the letters and do the reading for the others when it is necessary. Are there not people who can do these things? Your daughter reads well at the meetings of the Legion of Mary.'

'There are people, Father-priest. But there are some things that are better that a man should do for himself.'

'Ah, Mr Dandrade, this is not the simple matter that it seems to be. It involves a complete change, a complete break away from your traditional ways.'

The man from Kumaca played with the rim of his hat on his knee.

'We talk about it in Kumaca. We say the priest is a man with learning, and that he will help us,' the man said.

'I will help as much as I can. What do your people think?' Father Vincent asked.

'True, some think that the young men will leave the cocoa fields and sit on the bench in front of the shop and only read the newspapers. Some think that a school will cost money which Kumaca cannot afford. But everyone feels in his heart that it will be a great and wonderful thing to hear his son read a letter, and for himself to understand the words he has written down on paper for himself.'

'And your people, are they ready for this school?'

'I do not clearly know what you mean, Father-priest.'

'Are you prepared for the changes which a school in your midst is sure to bring about? There will be changes the consequences of which now we cannot even imagine.'

Paulaine Dandrade was a little disappointed with the priest now, and he showed it on his face. He said, 'Changes? But is not life a matter of changes, Father-priest? Look at me. My hair will not be for ever black. And does not the seed make another tree when it falls to the ground and mixes with the earth?'

'Your people are different, Mr Dandrade. They are ... well ... simple ... yes, unsophisticated. They have grown up in a tradition which is not easy to break, nor perhaps wise to break ... I have seen your beautiful festival at the time of Easter.'

'We in Kumaca are different to other people, Father-priest? And you do not think we should have a school? Eh?'

The man Paulaine Dandrade took up his hat in his two hands and prepared to stand. He looked for a moment at the priest, then he looked at the hat in his hands. He stood. The priest also stood.

'I do want to help you, Mr Dandrade,' the priest said.

'You want to help me, Father-priest? Is it hard for you to help me?'

'You take offence too quickly at what I say, Mr Dandrade. It is really not an easy decision to take, to build a school at Kumaca. Perhaps I will have to see the Bishop. It is not an easy decision.'

'Father-priest, if you cannot help then maybe I should go to see the Bishop and ask him. Where does he live that I may go to talk to him?'

'Mr Dandrade, please sit a moment.'

The man looked at the chair, fingered his hat, then he resumed his seat, sitting on the edge of the chair, his hat held ready in his hands, as if he were in a hurry to leave. The priest also took his seat.

'Kumaca,' said the priest, 'is simple and beautiful. Your people are good, honest, simple, hard-working, and in the season, God willing, your crop is good. Maybe you are not learned like the doctors and lawyers of the city, but you believe in the Virgin, and in the Father and in His Son who died for us all. You live happy, with your problems which are not too big for you to solve. Maybe it is a good thing that you are so cut off from the outside world.'

Paulaine looked into the eyes of the priest.

'The time will come, Father-priest, when the road from Valencia will be open, and there will be a different Kumaca. People will come and go as they do now between Valencia and Zanilla. I cannot stop that, Father-priest, you cannot stop it. It will happen.'

'Yes, it will happen.'

'And why you do not think our people good enough to learn to read and to write? Yet they go to Port-of-Spain, they come even here to Zanilla and are at the mercy of those who have the learning. They did not send me from Kumaca to beg, Father-priest. They ask me to get advice on how the school is to be built. But I go back to them to say that I do not have any advice on the school.'

'Their is much more to be considered in a school than the building,' Father Vincent said.

'That is why they send me to get advice. But maybe I better go to the Bishop. He is also a man of intelligence. Do you think he will help, Father-priest?'

'Believe me, Mr Dandrade, I am trying to help you.'

'But you talk only of the bad things that will come out of the building of the school. About the school itself, you say nothing. And I have made a long journey, and have only had my morning coffee.'

'I have not even had coffee,' the priest said.

'But you are a priest,' the man said.

Father Vincent smiled. He said, 'It is because I'm priest, and my responsibility great, that I must weigh carefully a matter before I make my judgment. But to speak directly about the building; if you want a Catholic school, then there are certain decisions which are the Church's and the Church's alone. Tell me, what lands do you have to build on?'

'I will give the lands myself, Father-priest.'

26

'And the building, do you think you can build it?'

'In Kumaca we build many good houses. We can build a good school.'

'If it is to carry the name of the Church, then we will pay the upkeep of the school, and we must provide the teachers, and of course, the building must be vested in the Church. It will belong in name to the Church.'

'You will help us then, Father-priest?'

'I am trying, Mr Dandrade. I hesitate to be definite for very good reasons. I have seen too much of this world corrupted, sir ... But do you follow what I am saying about the relationship of the school and the Church? Ah! and there is the matter of the teacher. He will have to travel. No, he will have to live in Kumaca. And where will he live? And an assistant might well be needed.'

'Is it possible to have a school with a teacher at Kumaca, Father-priest? That is what I want to know.'

'Patience, Mr Dandrade. There are still things to be discussed before it is decided.'

'Then you think the school could be built. Or you think no?'

Father Vincent got off his chair.

'I must think more of this. We will discuss it again when I come to the village on the Tuesday of Holy Week.'

Paulaine Dandrade got to his feet. He was not pleased around the eyes.

'I thank you, Father-priest. And I will tell the people of Kumaca the words you say. And we will wait and listen for you.'

'Very well,' the priest said. 'I will try my best. How was your crop this year?'

'Not too bad.'

'And the road, is it still very bad?'

'The weather is kind to the road. But it is still the donkeys. It is fortunate that the landslides are not very big.'

Paulaine Dandrade was leaving now, and Father Vincent detained him a little while.

'I see you care a great deal about Kumaca, eh, Mr Dandrade?'

The man didn't say anything. He looked at the priest.

Father Vincent said, 'Would you believe that I care too?'

'I am glad that you are going to help us, Father-priest,' Paulaine Dandrade said.

The tall, lean man stood a moment watching the priest. And Father Vincent felt a twinge of sadness in his heart, and he wished that he did not have such a man to deal with, because maybe the school should not be built in Kumaca, maybe it would not be good for the villagers. But how do you tell this to such a man? If he must say no, then he must have his *no* backed by the force of reason before which this man must bow. And maybe he would have to say no.

'Good morning, Father-priest.'

'Good morning, Mr Dandrade. Until the Tuesday of Holy Week.'

The priest stood and watched the man clutching his hat for a moment before he put it on his head and hastened with long strides through the door, then through the gate.

II

Holy Week had come now, and the blossoms of the poui were all gone from the hillsides. It was very quiet in the country between Valencia and Kumaca. For many days there had been no rain, and it was very dry, with crisp, fallen, still golden leaves on the ground. The weather was fine, with unseen birds singing, and with the wind and sunshine very gay with the tops of trees.

It was Tuesday, and Father Vincent was now making his quarterly journey to Kumaca to say the mass, and to do the baptisms. At this time of year the demands on the priests of the Church were heavy, and Father Vincent had to return to Zanilla that very night because there were many churches of importance in his parish which he had to visit during the Holy Week, and Easter.

With the priest were two acolytes, slim youngsters of thirteen or fourteen, and the fellow who owned the donkeys on which they were riding. He was a tense, hard man who could at times be very quiet, very poised and certain of himself, as if in some crude, rough way he had no need for anyone or anything. He travelled at the head of the small group, the priest behind him, and the two acolytes to the rear.

It was the first trip for both acolytes, and Father Vincent heard them behind him, talking excitedly to each other, their adolescent voices going suddenly and awkwardly over a range of notes. He did not pay much attention to them. Since he had had the talk with Paulaine Dandrade, he had been thinking of this matter of the school for Kumaca. At first he had been certain that it would not be in the best interest of the villagers, but then he thought that it might be better for them to have it, if they felt they needed it. But precisely because such an approach tended to dismiss, or disregard the many factors which he knew were involved, and as such was not a decision based on reason and knowledge, he rejected it, although as yet he had been unable to find strong enough acceptable reasons for his rejection. But in his heart he knew that he was right. Yet he was worried. He still had to explain to Mr Dandrade and the others.

The man riding in front of the priest, signalled him to stop; and he in turn lifted a hand and passed on the order to the acolytes. The man dismounted, and they did the same.

'Landslide. Wait here,' he said.

The track was very narrow at this point, and curved around the mountain. The man took the donkeys one by one and led them past the landslide, around the mountain. The priest watched him. He was a tough, squat man with a long grey whiskers. His back was kept very straight, and his legs were a little bandy. Benn was his name. When he had crossed all the donkeys, he returned and signalled the priest and the acolytes to follow him.

Loose earth had fallen away from the hillside, making the track very narrow and uncertain. If you placed your feet in a loose pocket of earth, you were likely to be swept, earth and all, down to the waiting precipice. The priest put his foot wherever Benn put his. They crossed very carefully, and without a word. Then they were on the other side where the donkeys had been tied, and Father Vincent felt that he should talk to the man.

'The landslide is not good,' the priest said.

'It is a landslide,' Benn said.

'It should be cleared. But I don't see how it can be done.'

The man did not say anything. He went over to where he had tied the donkeys, and began to unloose them.

'The donkeys seem much better this year,' the priest said. 'Which one had the swelling on its fetlock last year?'

The man pointed to one of the animals. He unloosed them all, and handed them over to their riders. But he did not mount yet. He began to walk, and the priest came abreast of him. They walked for a little while in silence.

'You never seem to talk much,' Father Vincent said.

'I talk,' the man said.

'Yes, they are much better,' the priest said, looking at the donkey he was leading.

'They all right,' Benn said.

'Do you work here all the time?'

'No.'

'You are also a gardener?'

The man shook his head.

'You live at Valencia, don't you?'

The man nodded. The priest had the impression that the man considered him a nuisance, but he persisted.

'What do you do when you are not working here?'

Benn had a slow, crisp way of speaking, as if he were very sure of himself.

'I go to Zanilla and get drunk. I get drunk Valencia too. But I prefer Zanilla. I do not know many people there. My money stretches much longer.'

'That is all?'

The man nodded.

'And how do you feel . . . afterwards . . .?'

'I do not know. I don't feel anyhow.'

'But still you do it? You go and spend your money on rum?'

The man didn't say anything.

'But you should know that that isn't good for you,' the priest said.

The man shrugged and muttered something to the donkey at his side.

'You do not attend church?'

'No.'

'I will pray for you.'

The man walked on without slackening his pace. The priest thought that he wasn't ever going to say anything.

30

'What will you pray, priest?' the man asked in a very gentle voice, not looking at Father Vincent.

'I will pray that you be not tempted by strong drinks,' the priest said, marvelling at the gentleness and the control in the man's voice.

Father Vincent almost slipped into a crack on the track. Just in time, he saw where he had been about to put his foot, and avoided the crack. It disconcerted him.

The man Benn spoke carefully, slowly; and he deliberately wanted to be gentle with the priest.

'Why will you pray that, priest?'

And Father Vincent, a little worried, and thinking how he had almost put his foot into a crack, and a little taken aback by the question and its tone, but realizing very quickly that such a question was somehow to be expected from such a man, and conscious of the acolytes listening behind him, answered with as much near-righteous dignity and tolerance as he could muster.

'It is my duty. As priest.'

'Your duty? No, priest,' Benn said, and began to walk faster.

Father Vincent gave no indication that he had noticed the increase in the man's pace. He simply stretched his own legs, and kept up with him. He realized that a subtle contest was on now.

'What do you mean?' Father Vincent asked.

The man, without turning or in any way inflecting his voice, said: 'That is not your duty. That is not the duty of any man or priest.'

And the priest: 'But how can you say that?'

'I say it because it is so.'

And the priest, exasperated both at the rudeness of the man and his own stubborn persistence (he should have left the man to his ignorance), and being caught in the subtle contest which his pride (which he should not have exhibited), allowed him to pretend to ignore and in fact caused him to pursue.

'I know you say it. But why?'

The man looked at him now, out of eyes hidden deep below greying brows.

'Who gives you the right, priest?'

'Who gives me the . . .? Who gives *me* . . .?'

Father Vincent turned from rising irritation to a tone at once distant, authoritative, and so cool that he marvelled secretly at the power of his soul, and felt that truly he was a priest. As to a little child, he spoke.

'When you pray, what is it you say?'

'I do not say anything.'

'When you pray, do you not say: Give us this day our daily bread. And lead us not into temptation ... And lead us not into temptation ...?'

The priest looked at the man, and he felt as if he were standing on a high hill which he had just climbed.

'That is not the way He said it. I do not believe that. No. I cannot.'

'What do you believe?'

'I believe, priest, that I am getting old, that soon someone else will take these donkeys across the hills. I believe that.'

'And lead us not into temptation ...' Father Vincent repeated.

Benn stopped walking.

'Priest. I believe that a man has need of his temptations as he has need of a woman. How else is a man a man if he is not tempted? If he is not proved? And these words you tell me, I do not see how He could say them.'

'You do not believe that the words were said?'

'No. We will ride now.'

Benn pulled himself up on the donkey, and he watched the others mount their animals. The priest did not let him get away. He rode at his side. The acolytes came behind.

'The Holy Scripture is our guide and our law,' the priest said. 'It is true and unchangeable.'

'Look, priest – in this Bible, Christ is the example for us, not so?'

'Of course he is.'

'All right. And he was tempted! Forty days and forty nights the Bible say. By Lucifer himself. Eh?'

'Yes,' Father Vincent said.

'Why, priest? Why?'

Before Father Vincent could speak, Benn was adding:

'And Peter was a great disciple. And before the cock crow three times, or maybe it was twice, I don't remember ... And he was tempted ... A man needs to be tempted, priest. Only then he is man.'

'But we are weak. The spirit is willing, but the flesh is weak. That is why we pray.'

'No. It is because we are weak we have need of our temptations.' So that the test will prepare us. So that you pass your test and go to a higher class. But you say, Lead me away from my test. I say, Lead me to my test, and let me pass my test.' Benn paused and smiled. 'But with me, priest, I am weak, and do not pass my test. I get drunk again, and I go back again and get drunk.'

Father Vincent didn't say anything for a long while.

'Then I will pray that you be strengthened to meet your temptations.'

'Yes, priest. You can pray that for me. And also pray it for yourself. Because all of us have our temptations to meet.'

And thinking in the silence now, the priest thought: Yes, I will also pray that for myself.

The morning continued dry and fine. They had to dismount twice again before they got to Kumaca where they were met by the church people, and taken to the house of Lucien, where in a shed adjoining the house, the priest heard the confession of those who were to receive Holy Communion, then he went with the acolytes to the place where there was a statue of the Virgin, and celebrated the mass out in the open. The Gospel he read was taken from Saint Mark:

But he cometh and findeth them sleeping, and said unto Peter, Simon, sleepest thou? Could'st not thou watch one hour?

Watch ye and pray, lest ye enter into temptation. The spirit truly is ready, but the flesh is weak.

After the mass Father Vincent was tired. He had tried to use the Gospel to convey something to the people; and though he had lifted up his voice and spread out his arms; though he had said many words, perhaps too many; at the end, he was not satisfied; and when he saw Benn's eyes staring from the congregation, he knew that he would have to surrender. For perhaps it was true that a man had need of his temptations.

Afterwards, with Paulaine Dandrade, Consantine Patron and others, he did not make any great resistance.

Paulaine Dandrade said that they would give the lands and would build the school and hand it over to the Church.

'You understand fully what you are doing?' Father Vincent asked rather tiredly.

Dardaine said, 'We understand, Father.'

'And you realize that it will now be the property of the Church, and as such will be governed by the Church?'

'We understand,' Paulaine Dandrade said.

'Very well. I will talk to the Bishop, and it will be settled. We will have to find a teacher who is willing to come up here. Where will he live?'

'He will get a place. We will build a fine house for our schoolmaster.'

'You must come and see me again after I have seen the Bishop.'

'We will come in about a month's time.'

'Very well.'

The priest looked at the eager faces before him. Ah! he was not happy in his heart. He remembered the words of the Gospel he had read a little while earlier. They would have had it anyway, he thought. The Bishop would agree. For he would say to the Bishop:

'Your Grace, the people need a school.'

And the Bishop, half-listening, would say: 'Fine, Father. Where?'

And he would say: 'In Kumaca, your Grace. They have given the lands to the Church, and will build with their own labour and materials.'

The Bishop would say: 'Fine, Father, fine.'

'And they would like us to take over the school, and provide a schoolmaster, and the management of the school.'

And the Bishop listening now, would lean forward and say: 'But that is excellent, Father. You have my permission to go on immediately. This is indeed excellent.'

And he, Father Vincent, would not have it within him to articulate his fears, to raise the questions of the simplicity of the people and the possibility of their destruction. So they would have their school. And again he remembered the words of the Gospel he had read a while before.

34

Chapter Three

I

It had turned dusk now, and mosquitoes were singing in the kitchen. Outside, the rain had ceased and water was dripping off wet leaves, making intimate, dark whispers in the cocoa fields and surrounding forest where frogs were croaking, and cigales hissing their teeth. There would be no moon, and Kumaca would begin another damp, gloomy August night.

In the kitchen, Christiana, the only daughter of Paulaine Dandrade, had just finished preparing the evening's meal, and was putting things in order before she went into the house where the family ate. With her was Humphy, her youngest brother, a fat boy of eight, with big bright eyes and a great appetite. He had finished playing before the others, had washed himself, and now sat on the bench, following the movements of his sister with his huge eyes, as she tidied up the place. He was hungry, and had been very patient, didn't say a word, just sat and watched her. Now and again his eyes would stray over to the table where lay the three massive coconut bakes, the bowl of saltfish buljol with tomatoes and a bit of green pepper, and the large pot of chocolate and goat's milk.

Humphy sat unmoving, watched Christiana pour some chocolate into a large enamel cup which she placed near to the dying fire in the fireside where she already had a smaller cup with strong black coffee. Then she was ready to go inside.

'That is for Papa, eh, Christiana?' Humphy said, saying the obvious, feeling that he could talk now that the time for eating was so near.

'Yes, for Papa,' she said. 'Let us go inside. Call the others.'

Humphy jumped off the bench, sped to the door of the kitchen, and reeled off the names of his brothers.

'Manuel, Sonny, Henry, Albert. Ready!'

'Help me,' Christiana said, giving the small boy the bowl with the saltfish buljol. She herself took the bakes and the pot of chocolate. The cups and plates were inside.

Christiana fixed the table for her brothers, and as they sat down to eat, she went to light the lamp. She wondered whether it would rain again. She hoped that it didn't rain, because her father was walking up from Valencia that very night. She cleaned the sooty shade, then lit the lamp. Mosquitoes swarmed in the room, making their thin, maddening, piercing sounds.

'Please, Manuel, when you finish eat, make some smoke for these mosquitoes,' she said.

Manuel was the one before her. He was seventeen. In the wet season when the mosquitoes were most vicious, it was necessary to make a fire, then pack green bush atop it so that there would be lots of smoke. This drove the mosquitoes away.

'The bush wet outside,' Manuel said. 'But I will see what I do. You not eating now?'

'I will wait a little for Papa. It makes him feel good for one of us to sit down and eat with him.'

A gust of wind came through the window, like a strong puff of breath, startling the lamp, sending the flames jumping. Christiana went to the window, but there she paused and looked outside. She could feel the damp air on her cheeks, and off in the village, she saw the points of lights – lamps lit in houses around – and heard, above the forest-sounds and the dripping of water off the leaves, the sound of music, and knew as she listened that it was Pedro Assivero playing on his bamboo flute. And she thought:

> The boy who is full of jokes and mischief.
> I danced with him at Easter time and he stepped often
>   on my toes.
> It is quiet outside and all the birds are not sleeping.
> In the darkness he is playing on his bamboo flute.
> I went down to the river one day and he was waiting.
> He showed me a young squirrel he had caught with his
>   hands.
> He was sad that I did not accept it.
> It is not good for girls my age to take things from boys.
> I can hear the notes of his flute climb over the yellow
>   pouis.

My heart is melted like a river and flows around inside
me.
Why is he playing in the dark?
If he is such a funny boy why am I listening to his
flute?

Christiana turned from the window. She had forgotten that she had
come to close it from the wind. She saw Manuel looking at her.

'Did you bring in the goats, Manuel?' she asked automatically.

'I tell Henry to do it. You bring them in, Henry?'

'Yes, Mr Manuel. I bring them in. You are always telling Henry to
bring them in. Soon I will go from here, then I will see who will bring
them in.'

'Where you will go?' Manuel asked.

'I will go to the city where there are streetlights, and I will ride in
the tramcars. I will buy many fine things in the shops, and when I
come back to Kumaca, you will not recognize me.'

'So you will come back, then?'

'But I will not stay.'

'When you come back, will you take me back with you, Henry?'
Humphy the smallest asked.

Christiana laughed.

'He himself has not left yet, and you ask him to take you.'

The others, Manuel and Sonny, laughed, and even Henry and
Humphy joined in after a little while.

Henry said, 'This place is very lonely on a night like this.

'Soon we will have the school,' Christiana said. 'Then the place will
not be so lonely.'

The wind came again through the window and threatened the lamp.
Christiana moved to the window, and as she leaned to pull it in, she
heard again the sound of Pedro's flute on the night, and recalled that
she had come earlier to do just what she was doing now. Then she
saw the torchlight searching in the darkness of the track that led up
to the house, and for some added reason, she was glad that her father
was coming home.

'Papa!' she cried, leaving the window unclosed, and turning to the
boys who had just finished their meal.

As a man, they all, with the exception of Manuel jumped to their legs and sped outside to meet their father. Manuel went outside to make the fire and to get the bush to make the smoke against the mosquitoes. Christiana herself cleared the things from the table and carried them into the kitchen.

She was in the kitchen when her father came, surrounded by the boys. He was not wet, and he held many parcels in his hands. He stood in the doorway. His face was tired, but he was smiling.

'Ah, girl, you still in the kitchen, eh?' he said.

'I am fixing the coffee for you, Papa.'

He smacked his lips, and nodded.

'Yes,' he said with satisfaction and moved to sit down. 'Where is Manuel?'

'He is outside making smoke for the mosquitoes. Did you see the priest, Papa?'

'Yes, girl. I see the priest. Everytime he is fighting with himself, like he is watching a man dying, who he has wounded. I say, Priest-father, there is nothing to be afraid of. He fights with himself all the time.'

Christiana poured the coffee into a tea-cup and handed it to her father.

'Is it hot enough, Papa?'

Paulaine Dandrade sipped.

He said, 'Good.'

Then drank the remainder in one smooth swallow.

'Good. Now let us go inside and see what I bring for everybody. Call Manuel too. And you come, Christiana.'

'I am bringing your supper, Papa.'

The boys followed their father into the house, and Christiana followed with the supper.

Her father was saying: 'This is for you, Sonny. And this for Henry. Albert, this is yours. Manuel, come and see if this jersey can fit you. If it too small you will give it to Henry, eh? Humphy, boy, this is yours. Where is Christiana? Come, Christiana. This dress, the lady at the store says it is very good. I myself find it very pretty. What do you think?'

'It is nice, Papa.'

'The jersey fit you, Manuel? Let me see. Ah, yes. It good. Is it not good?'

'It is good, Papa.'

'Good. And look what I also bring for you.'

'What is it, Papa?'

The boys crowded around their father who was now searching in his bag. He brought out one book, and he looked from one face to the other.

'I bring a book for everybody. For you to read out of.'

He handed the first book to Manuel and dug into the bag for another.

'Thank you, Papa,' Manuel said, taking the book and looking at it, not opening it.

'Now that the school is to open, every man will have to learn to read. Christiana will show you what you do not know.'

Each of the boys took his book, they all turned the pages rapidly. Only Manuel, who was not easily excited, put his book on the cabinet, and turned to go outside.

'What is it, Manuel?'

'I am going to put some more bush on the fire, Papa.'

Manuel went outside, and the smaller boys went in a corner to compare pictures in the different books. Christiana had put the supper on the table, and now she sat down with her father, to eat.

'The rain did not wet you, Papa?'

'It sprinkle me a little. I had to shelter. You don't see how I reach late. You like the dress I buy for you, in truth? The lady in the store at Zanilla say it is a very good dress.'

'I like it.'

'Good. You will wear it when the school is opening. You know we *must* have a fête, and the music and maybe dancing when the school is opening.'

'When will that be, Papa?'

'The priest say he can come on the twenty-fourth of this month. Today is the seventh. We have time to prepare a grand fête. The priest and the schoolmaster will come, and the priest will bless the school.'

'Did you see the schoolmaster, Papa?'

'I did not see him. I wanted to see him, but I will see him when he comes with the priest. The priest says he is a good man. The priest himself is not a bad fellow. Coward a little bit but not a bad fellow. I do not understand why he is so afraid. You know why, I think, girl?'

Christiana looked the question at her father.

'He is afraid that we change too much, that we become like the people of the towns. He thinks we will go bad, and do little work, and drink much rum, and gamble, and leave the cocoa to rot in the fields. I say to him, Father-priest, life is change . . . I do not think he is a bad fellow. Coward . . . Ah, this buljol and bake is fine tonight. But I can also take a drink of rum for the weather, and because I feel happy inside my heart now that I know the school is to be opened and we already have a schoolmaster.'

'I will get it for you, Papa.'

Christiana rose and went to the cabinet and took out the bottle of rum.

'Manuel-boy, your smoke is stifling me. It is the mosquitoes you want to kill, not so?' Paulaine Dandrade called to his son.

'I hear you, Papa. I will take off some of the bush,' Manuel called back.

'Good. Come in from the cold, and take a drink with your papa. And you boys, come. A little bit is good for the worms hiding in your belly.'

Christiana brought with the rum a jug of water and glasses for everybody.

Paulaine himself distributed the liquor.

'This is for you, Humphy. And this is enough for you, Mister Albert. No. I throw too much for you, Henry. But go on. You are going to sleep in a little while. Sonny, you take this.'

Manuel was at his father's elbow, and Paulaine looked around, took the bottle in his hand and looked at Manuel.

'Here. Pour for yourself a drink, my son. And sit down and let us talk,' he said, giving Manuel the bottle.

Manuel took the bottle, looked at it suspiciously, then poured a small drink for himself.

'Manuel, the schoolmaster is coming. The school will be open on the twenty-fourth of this month.'

Paulaine poured his own drink.

He said, 'Let us drink. You sure you do not want, Christiana? Take a little touch, girl.'

Christiana allowed herself to be persuaded, brought a glass and poured a few drops into it.

'Now, let us all drink,' Paulaine said.

They drank, all of them making unpleasant faces, except Paulaine himself, and Humphy.

'You, Mister Humphy, will be a drunkard,' Paulaine said jovially.

'Manuel-boy, I do not know why you do not like school And it is for all-you I do this. It is for the children of Kumaca this idea work in my head. And we build the school We do it. It was not easy for the priest either. Because he has an idea we do not need the school. Everytime I go to see him he is fighting with himself. But if something is to happen, by God, how can a man even if he is a priest stop it. I know we need this school. I know that a man must live in his times. And I feel happy that we get the priest to agree, and we have with our own hands built the school. But it can benefit only if you use it. Yet there are some of you who say you do not like school. I do not understand it.

'Manuel-boy, look at Kumaca. It is only high woods and cocoa trees now, and not much different to when I was a boy. And Valencia was the same thing. And the track to Valencia was even better when I was young. And Zanilla was not bright, and did not have lights and the tall buildings you see now, even the road did not have pitch on them. A man did not have to know to read then. You take up your cutlass and you go on the estate. But now a man must know things. If you want to go to Zanilla or Arima, or if you want to go to Port-of-Spain, you cannot go like a fool now. The world is not the same place it used to be, and a man must keep up with the world. I could read and write a little. The people who can read and write will say that you not bound to learn these things, but they already know to do them.

'You have to care about things, Manuel-boy. You have to care to improve yourself not only for you but for the place you live in, for the world you live in. A man does have to carry the world with him. It sounds funny to your ears, but it is true. And now you hear cigales crying all over Kumaca, and monkey bawling, and birds, but just now

41

it will be streetlights like in Zanilla, and motor-car horns blowing for you to get out the way. I agree a man can live without ever writing his name, or reading a letter, but that not enough, boy. Your big brother leave and gone in the city, and he could read a little bit, but what can he do? What work he could get, eh? And a man does have to learn things in the world, because it is not only cocoa and wild beast in the bush that in the world, and cutting down forest trees, and working the bull pulling out the logs. And you young. That is what you have more than anything else. And we spend our time in Kumaca. Now it is very quiet, but just now, maybe even now it too quiet for your hot blood. And what you know to do when you leave here? Books have plenty for people to learn. And I sit down here, and know that the world bigger than Kumaca – in fact, sometimes I feel that Kumaca not even in the world. But with the school now, and the children learning, Kumaca will be in the world. Maybe you ask, why Kumaca should be in the world? It is a good question. But then a man can ask why he in the world at all. And that is a good-good question too, eh?'

Paulaine Dandrade poured himself another drink. He said:

'I talk too much tonight. But a man is right to talk to his children. If anything happen to me, is to you, Manuel, the others looking, because Christiana is a girl, and soon maybe she go to make some man happy. So I talk to you. You understand now why I talk so much to you? And why all the children should go to the school?'

Manuel said, 'I understand, Papa.'

But Paulaine Dandrade looked at his son, and although he wanted to feel that the boy understood, he felt that he had just said the words to satisfy him. And he thought: Perhaps he is yet too young, and yet lazy.

And he thought: To think that my own biggest son does not understand.

And he thought: Maybe when the school is opened and the schoolmaster comes, he will understand.

And this last hope, Paulaine Dandrade held in his heart. But he would see. It was not long to wait.

Chapter Four

I

It was finally the twenty-fourth day of the month, and the rain begun since three hours after daybreak, now at mid-afternoon still beat furiously upon the galvanized iron roofing of the new schoolhouse at Kumaca. Outside in the grey-green mistiness, trees reared their heads like wild horses, as the wind raced roaring through the forest. In the schoolhouse, the villagers stood around in small, weary-faced groups imprisoned by the incessant rain and with their best clothes on, waiting in a vain hopefulness for the priest and the schoolmaster to turn up. They listened to the rain and the wind outside, and had no taste for the food they had prepared for the occasion. Even the musicians had no heart to play their instruments. Only Paulaine Dandrade standing at the front door, with his tight, black jacket and fat, green tie, kept muttering to himself: 'They will come. They will come,' like a man talking too loudly in his sleep. He had been the one chiefly responsible for the preparations, and now he felt very alone, fidgety, vexed and aggressively hopeful. They had to come.

Near to Paulaine at the door was a group of drinking men: Miguel, the great trainer of cocks, Sibley his cousin, and the brothers Santo and Ramon Pampoon, all in their best clothes and sad, two-toned, newly-shaven faces. They had been drinking since their arrival at the schoolhouse, and were a little drunk now.

'This rain,' Miguel, the great one with the cocks, said gravely. 'It is a bad sign, this rain.'

As if that were a signal, one of the Pampoon brothers poured himself a drink, very solemnly, and passed the bottle to Miguel.

Dardain the shopkeeper and Consantine Patron had been in a corner, talking to old Lucien who was sitting on a chair, and now they left Lucien and came over to where Paulaine was standing by the door.

Dardain looked through the door.

'Still falling heavy,' he said. 'What you think Paulaine?'

Before Paulaine could reply, Miguel, the great one with the fighting cocks, found himself at the edge of the company, and said very gravely:

'This rain is a bad-bad sign.'

Consantine Patron, also dressed in his best clothes that fitted him well, but unshaven, and with his fountain pens clipped on the pocket of his brown jacket, pushed his hand into a pocket.

'It is a blessing,' he said in a cynical tone, turning and looking outside.

'Can't tell when last I see weather so,' Dardain said.

'They will come,' Paulaine said very softly, as if he didn't quite believe what he was saying.

'Maybe tomorrow,' Dardain said. 'And all the food spoiling. All the food, and nobody eating.'

'A bad sign,' Miguel intoned.

'They will come,' Paulaine said a little more assertively. 'I walk through worse rain than this already.'

'But this is the priest and the schoolmaster,' Dardain said.

Paulaine said: 'They must come. We make the preparations, they must come.'

Miguel said: 'Plenty food to eat, much liquor to drink: if they come, they come. I going to have a good time. Fête!'

Paulaine Dandrade looked at the rain falling outside.

'One time in a storm, and with trees falling, I walk from Valencia to here. Eh. Remember the time, Dardain? House top and all the wind blow away.'

Dardain said: 'Is not you to blame why the rain fall.'

'Is a bad sign,' Miguel said, turning now to join his own group and Sibley, who was handing him the bottle with the mountain dew.

Dardain said: 'We better take a drink. I have a whisky in the room of the schoolmaster. Come. You worrying yourself for what, Paulaine? If the rain to stop, is the father-priest to stop it. If he cannot pray and stop it, what can you do? Let us go and take one. Come. You will take one, Paulaine? We make a good preparation, but the rain fall. What can we do, eh? Come, Consantine.'

'Maybe the band should play,' Consantine Patron said.

'Yes, they should play. It will not be so sad. Come, let us go for the whisky in the room of the schoolmaster. They say a good end comes from a bad beginning,' Dardain said.

'I think I will take a drink,' Paulaine said.

Dardain said, 'You now talking. But let me first go and tell the band to play the music, and let the people dance and have a good time. They must eat the food before it goes to waste. The rum will not spoil.'

'Yes, let us have the music,' Paulaine said.

'I go to advise them. Wait for me,' Dardain said.

Consantine Patron turned to Paulaine.

'You really think they will come?'

'They have to come,' Paulaine said.

So now the band struck up, and Pedro Assivero, who from a distance had been looking at Christiana the daughter of Paulaine Dandrade, walked across the door to her. Half-way across he changed his mind and his direction and went instead to where some boys of about his own age were having drinks and talking.

'Give me a drink,' Pedro said.

They gave him the bottle and a glass. He took the drink and remained with the boys, not saying anything, listening to their joking. Now and again he would glance across at Christiana. He took another drink.

'I go to dance now,' he said.

'Go on,' one of the boys said.

The others looked at him, and they all laughed.

'It is no joke. I am going,' Pedro said. 'Yet you laugh.'

'Go on,' the same fellow said.

They all looked at him and laughed again.

'Give me a drink,' Pedro said.

The bottle was handed to him, and the glass.

'No. I do not need it.'

He resumed the bottle and the glass. The boys looked at him and laughed.

'You are foolish fools,' he said.

'Look, she is looking at you,' one of them said.

The fellows laughed.

Pedro said, 'Do not speak of her with your mouth, if you do not want a fight.'

'He is much in love,' the biggest fellow in the crowd said.

'I better go from you, or there will be a fight,' Pedro said.

Pedro did not yet own a jacket, but he had borrowed one of his father's ties. He was wearing a fine long-sleeved shirt which he had bought at the shop of Dardain. Before he realized what he was doing, he found himself walking towards Christiana. There was no possibility of turning back. And now he stood mute, confused before her. The music was playing. Her hair was combed up on the top of her head, and her eyes were large and were always asking a question. Brown eyes. He asked her to dance. He couldn't tell if he had spoken. An eternity. Then she was in his arms. He saw the boys looking at him. They moved along the floor for a while.

'This rain will not stop,' he said.

'It is falling,' she said.

Stop. Pedro looked at the decorations on the walls of the schoolhouse: the mountain fern, the balisier flowers, the palm leaves, and the anthurium lilies. Danced. His lips touched her brow. Touched. He fell out of step. Struggled to get back in time with the music.

'Am I dancing good, and not mashing your foot?'

'You are not mashing my foot,' she said.

'Did you know I wanted to dance with you?'

Silence.

'I was afraid to walk across . . .'

'Why?'

'It is when I see you. My heart comes into my mouth, and feathers tickle inside my chest.'

'Why does this happen to you?'

'I cannot answer . . . Do you hear me play my flute?'

'I hear sometimes.'

'I play my flute for you. Do you like how I play?'

'It is very nice how you play.'

The music stopped, and Pedro walked with her back to her seat.

'Will you go to the school?' Pedro asked.

'Yes.'

46

'I hear that already you can read and write.'

'It is true.'

'Then you can be a teacher in the school.'

'You must have much learning to be a teacher. I do not have that much learning. Will you go to the school?'

'Next month I will have twenty years,' Pedro said. 'And yet I will go to the school. Does it take long to learn to write the letters and to spell the words?'

'Some people do not take long,' she said.

'But you can write and spell. They say that you can write almost as well as your father. Does it take long for you to do these things?'

'It did not take very long.'

'I will have to learn very quick. I have to learn to write very well. You want for me to tell you why?'

She was smiling.

'You can tell me.'

'It is for a very serious occasion I must write a letter,' Pedro said.

'Is that serious?'

'I must write this letter to the father of the girl that I . . . that I . . . love.'

'Oh!'

'You look serious now,' he said.

'I am not serious.'

'You would like to know the girl whose father I must write?'

'No. No,' she said, quickly.

'Then I will not tell you. Do you want to dance again with me?'

'I can dance, yes.'

She stood and he took her hand and led her to the floor. Pedro was as light as a breeze, and inside him bells were ringing, and stars bursting in his chest.

The rain did not cease until late evening, and then Paulaine Dandrade was forced to admit that the priest and schoolmaster would not be coming again that day. It was very sad, with the villagers stale and quiet and some of the men drunk and unhappy. Although some of the women carried home meat, much of the food that had been prepared had to be thrown to the dogs. Pedro Assivero walked home thinking of Christiana, and feeling in his heart, indeed in his whole self, a new, clean pain. He was so happy, he was stupid.

He arrived home and went into the room which he shared with his smaller brother Robert. Robert was lying on the bed with his eyes closed. For a fortnight now he had been stricken with a strange disease which had given him fever, and had made his legs so numb that he couldn't walk. There was no doctor in Kumaca, and the warm baths ordered by Papa Marcelle, the bush doctor, had caused no improvement in his condition. He had terrible pains in his legs and did not sleep well at nights. They would have to carry him to the doctor at Zanilla. Now, as Pedro entered the room, he opened his eyes. Pedro went and sat on the edge of the bed.

'How do you feel, Robert?'

'I feel a little better, Pedro. The pain comes and goes now. Tell me, how did the schoolmaster look?'

'There was so much rain. He did not come. Did you ever see rain so?'

'I lie here on my bed, and listen to it. And the wind was very strong.'

'It was too much rain,' Pedro said, bending to undo his shoelaces.

'And you, Pedro. What happen with you? You are so not yourself.'

'I am myself, Robert.'

'Did you see the girl Christiana? And did you dance with her and say the words you had made up in your mind to say?'

'I did not say the very words, but I danced with her.'

'Many times you danced with her? I could hear the band playing from here.'

'I danced three times with her.'

'Only?'

'I talked with her also. She is very nice, Robert.'

'You made good talk, eh, Pedro?'

'Yes. She say that it is not too difficult to learn to read and write. Soon I will write the letter to her father.'

'You will write the letter yourself, Pedro?'

'I cannot write it now, I know. Soon I will learn when I go to the school.'

48

'I want to go to the school, Pedro. I will learn very well.'

'You will learn very quick, Robert.'

You think I will learn very quick, Pedro?'

'I know it. But first you must get better.'

'I do not know when I will get better. I just lie here, and the pain comes and goes and comes again.'

'We will have to take you to the doctor at Zanilla, in the hospital there.'

'It will be too painful to travel. In my imagination already it pains.'

'We will be careful with you. If you travel on a good donkey it will not be too bad.'

'Sometimes I feel myself so tired, Pedro.'

'That is because you are weak.'

'And sometimes I am very, very frightened.'

'You will get well, Robert.'

'Sometimes I am very afraid, and I say, now if it was Pedro lying here, he would not be afraid. Would you be afraid, Pedro?'

'I would be afraid a little. Not much. If our father had money, he could ask the doctor to come up here to look at you. But it would cost so much, I myself cannot think of the sum.'

'Our father has no money. If I do not get well soon, I will have to go down by the donkey.'

'You will get well, Robert.'

'I hope so. I am happy that you talk with Christiana, and dance with her.'

'She is very nice. And to write that letter to her father, I would go to school a hundred times. And I do not know what else would make me go. Come now, you better go to sleep.'

'Yes. I wish that tomorrow I could go to see when the schoolmaster comes. You think they will come tomorrow?'

'Perhaps, if it doesn't rain,' Pedro said.

II

There was no rain on the following day, yet neither priest nor schoolmaster turned up. So now it was a cool fine afternoon that same week, with the she-goat chewing its cud under the mango tree, ground doves alighting and strutting around in the sunshine, pecking among pebbles and grass in the yard near the cocoa house of Paulaine Dandrade. Humphy, the youngest son of Paulaine, was sitting half-naked on the doorstep, swinging his legs, watching the doves in the sunshine and thinking: Wish I could have one to hold. He knew that as soon as he moved, they would fly up and away.

His father and other brothers had gone to the cocoa field to cutlass the grass and to gather firewood. Christiana was in the kitchen, lighting the coalpot in preparation to ironing clothes. In a little while she would call him to fan the fire. He sat waiting for her call. He had just eaten, his belly was full, and he didn't know what else to do with himself. He wished he had gone with the others. Suddenly he decided. He eased off the step, the doves did not fly up. He picked up a stone, and now he looked at the doves. He didn't want to hit them. He watched them, the stone held ready in his hand. He didn't want them to fly away. It was almost impossible to catch one. Then he drew back his hand and threw the stone. The doves flew away. He went back and sat on the steps. He scratched his head and tried to puzzle it out. Soon Christiana would call him to fan the fire, and he would go. He was the smallest.

He sat uneasily, waiting for her call. Farther down the yard, the ground doves were resuming cautiously. Even if he got one, he would have to get a cage for it.

'Humphy,' Christiana called.

He knew that he was being called to fan the fire, and he answered very reluctantly.

'Yes.'

'The fire,' she said.

'Coming,' he said.

He was raising himself lazily from the step when out of the corners of his eyes, he saw the doves fly up. Looking down the yard to the path that led up to the house, he saw two men approaching, and for a moment remained motionless watching with wide-open eyes, because in all his life he had never seen such a man as the one who came riding on the donkey.

'Boy!' Christiana called.

50

But Humphy, gazing at the man on the donkey, did not hear her.

'Humphy!' Christiana shouted.

'Yes,' he answered tonelessly.

'You cannot hear me calling you to fan the fire, boy?'

'Somebody coming, Christiana.'

'Who?'

'One is Pedro . . . and . . .'

'Pedro! And who, Humphy?'

'Pedro and . . . and the governor,' the boy said, his round eyes fixed on the man. He jumped off the steps and stole around behind the kitchen where he remained hiding, watching the visitors come up to the house.

In the kitchen, Christiana, thrown into consternation at the mention of the name Pedro, did not know that her brother had stolen off. She was busy clasping and unclasping her hands. Then she heard Pedro's voice.

'Good evening, Mr Paulaine.'

Why did her heart thump so loudly and so fast? She went to the door of the kitchen. She clasped her hands, and with an effort lifted her eyes to Pedro's.

'Good evening. Papa is not home,' she said.

'I bring the schoolmaster to see him,' Pedro said, his face quite serious.

And now she glanced at the man who had dismounted from the donkey, became aware of his large eyes behind spectacles, felt the eyes going over her like hands, grabbed and held the edges of her dress which was open at the side.

'Good day, I am your schoolmaster. I am looking for Mr Dandrade. Your father, isn't he?'

The man's voice was low and frighteningly personal, as if he were alone with her. He was younger than her father, and younger perhaps even than Consantine Patron. He wore a suit with a striped tie, and a grey felt hat. She could understand why Humphy had called him the governor. The men in Kumaca never, never dressed so well.

'Yes, sir.'

'Fine. I do want to get into that little house you have provided for me.'

'I will send and call my father,' Christiana said. 'He is in the garden. Humphy!'

The small boy came slowly from behind the kitchen, his eyes fixed on the schoolmaster's black shoes.

'Come, little man. You are not afraid of me, are you?' he said, making a step in the boy's direction.

Humphy didn't say anything.

'You will soon be coming to my school, won't you? Won't he be coming to the school?' he asked, turning to the girl.

'Yes, sir.'

'And you will come also?'

She nodded and looked away from his eyes. She did not like to meet his eyes.

'Go and call Papa. Tell him the schoolmaster is here.'

Humphy made a slow, crooked line with his big toe, on the ground.

'He is the schoolmaster?' he asked, looking with new eyes at the man.

'I am the schoolmaster. Now, be off with you, little man. What is your name?'

The boy did not wait to answer. He ran off. The schoolmaster's eyes were again on Christiana.

She answered, 'His name is Humphy.'

'Humphy?' he asked, wrinkling his brows. 'And yours?'

'I am Christiana.'

'Christiana!' He sounded the name on his lips.

'Would you like to sit down? I have the ironing to do. Papa will be back in a little while.'

'Oh, you are the housewife! We must not keep the housewife from her work, must we?' he said, turning to Pedro who did not say anything.

'Rather cool out here. I don't mind sitting right here.'

'I'll get the chairs,' Christiana said.

'Please do,' he said, bowing lightly.

'I will help you, Christiana,' Pedro said.

She smiled and nodded as he joined her to get the chairs from the house.

52

'Fine young lady,' the schoolmaster said in his deep voice, looking at the form of the girl disappearing through the door of the kitchen. He was seated now and Pedro was at his side.

Pedro didn't say anything. Smiled.

'You will be attending the school too, eh, young man?'

'Yes, sir.'

'Good ... I had a hard journey today. You certainly need a road through from Valencia.'

'Yes, sir.'

'You have never had a school here, have you?'

'No, sir.'

The schoolmaster cocked his head to one side, and reached into his trousers pocket for a handkerchief to mop the two drops of perspiration that had appeared on his forehead.

'Ah! We have some work ahead of us.'

He touched the knot of his tie, and shook his head reflectively.

'We have some work ahead of us,' he repeated.

Then, hurrying up the path, came Mr Paulaine Dandrade, the long sleeves of his trousers flapping, making giant steps, out-distancing his sons.

'That will be Mr Dandrade,' the schoolmaster said.

'Yes,' Pedro said, rising to leave now.

'Wait. Let me see,' said the schoolmaster, himself rising, putting a hand into a breast pocket of his jacket and drawing out a leather wallet. He removed a sixpence piece.

'Take this.'

'No, thanks, sir.'

'Come on, take it, boy.'

'No, thanks,' said Pedro, and watched him replace the coin in his wallet.

Mr Dandrade had come up now. He was still struggling to catch his breath.

'Good evening, Mr Schoolmaster.'

'My name is Winston Warrick. How are you?' the schoolmaster said, presenting a hand to shake.

'I am Paulaine Dandrade. My daughter let you stay out here?' he asked, a note of mild censure in his tone, looking at the chairs.

'It was quite cool out here, and I asked to remain here,' the schoolmaster said.

'Well, we can go inside now. Pedro, how are you, boy?'

'I am well, thanks, Mr Paulaine. I am going now. Good evening, Mr Paulaine, Schoolmaster.'

And to Christiana, who had appeared at the door of the kitchen now, he said good evening.

'Good evening, Pedro.'

Pedro went down the path, slowly. He knew that it didn't make sense looking back at the house, still, he looked back. He was just about to turn into the track that would take him home when he so heard his name called. He looked back. It was Manuel, the son of Mr Paulaine. He waited.

'What is it?'

'My father asks you to help me tell the people that the schoolmaster is here. He wants to have a meeting at the school this very evening to say a few words of welcome.'

'I will do it. Let us go,' said Pedro.

'Yes. Soon it will make dusk. And we must remember to ask Mr Dardain to lend his gas lamp from the shop to light up the school.'

'We will not forget that. Let us go quick now.'

The schoolhouse was packed that night. In all his life, Paulaine Dandrade could not recall one time when he had had a better feeling flowing inside his heart. And he felt like he wanted to shake hands with all the men, and to kiss all the women, gathered there at the schoolhouse. His only regret was that Old Lucien was ailing and could not attend, and that the priest was not there to see how gladly the people received the schoolmaster.

Paulaine Dandrade knew that it was no good him trying to put into words the feeling inside him, knew that it was unjust of a man of himself to attempt to speak on an occasion when his heart was so full with gladness. But they called him to speak, and he wanted everyone to feel as he felt, to feel good, and beautiful and clean, and glad.

He said: 'I cannot tell how I feel glad in my heart here tonight. I will not try. We have this school now, and we have a schoolmaster now. We have worked hard and with our own hands have built the school. We must feel proud. We can learn very much, and our children must learn ... No, I cannot talk tonight. I must thank the schoolmaster, and I agree to give him my cooperation. I hope he will like the place, and he will have a good stay. More now, I cannot say.'

Ah, you are a woman, he thought, feeling the fullness in his eyes. Your eyes water with happiness.

Dardain was able to speak. He said that he too was happy to welcome the schoolmaster. He had willingly supported the villagers and had even that night loaned his gas lamp, and closed his shop to be at the meeting which was a great occasion in the history of Kumaca. He pledged his support and that of the villagers. The schoolmaster could always depend on him in any move aimed at bettering the village. He knew that there were other speakers who would like to say something, so he would take his seat.

Consantine Patron with his two fountain pens clipped to his breast pocket was silent. He did not get up to speak when Paulaine invited anyone who wanted to say anything. He sat still and listened to the schoolmaster reply.

He was happy to be there. He was greatly touched by the interest displayed by the villagers in absenting themselves from their homes at such an hour to welcome him into their midst. He pledged his cooperation. There was much to be done in the village, and with his experience, he knew that he could lift Kumaca out of its present poor state. The people should realize that the world was progressing, and that education was the key to progress. No one should feel himself too big to learn, and should not be afraid to enrol as a pupil in the school. He would have many more opportunities, he hoped, to address them, but for the moment, he wanted to offer his heartfelt thanks for the very moving welcome he had received.

Consantine Patron listened to the applause of the villagers, then watched the villagers hurrying forward to shake hands with the schoolmaster. He himself was dragged by Dardain and presented to the schoolmaster, but there was such a group of people around that it was a very brief and insignificant meeting for which he was not sorry.

Later when the crowd had thinned out and he was alone with Paulaine Dandrade, the schoolmaster said:

'I must thank you especially, Mr Dandrade.'

'It is nothing. I feel happy for the village. I hope you find your house comfortable. We will have to get someone to wash and cook for you, because you do not have a family. We will have to talk more about that.'

'Yes,' the schoolmaster said. 'For the moment, I think I will be quite comfortable. Your daughter, did you not say that she could read and write?'

'Better than me, even, she does these things,' Paulaine said.

'Then I would like to interview her. I would need an assistant.'

'Do you think she is good enough?'

'If you will send her to see me, I can find out if she is suitable,' the schoolmaster said.

'I will send her to see you, then. Good night, Mr Schoolmaster.'

'Good night, Mr Dandrade.'

Part Two

Chapter Five

I

Just past the landslide at the bend in the narrow track that wound like a clock's spring through the mountains between Valencia and Kumaca, Benn, who was taking the priest and two acolytes to Kumaca, pulled the donkey upon which he was riding to a stop, and with slow, unsteady movements got off its back, and threw himself full length upon the ground.

The priest who had been riding some distance behind him, now rode up.

'What is the matter?'

Benn rolled over, pulled himself up and rested upon his elbows. It was a cool day, but perspiration like a bunch of green sea grapes stood on his forehead, and his black face lined like an old accordion was twisted with a deep pain that seemed to be mastering him.

'I am drunk, priest. That is why we stop.'

'Oh!' the priest exclaimed almost inaudibly.

He signalled the acolytes who had ridden up in Indian file behind him, to dismount, and he himself got off the donkey he was riding.

It was the last week of December, with Christmas three days gone. The weather was fine for that time of year: sky bare of dark clouds, sunshine shining white through the treetops. All around it was quiet and very green. Butterflies hovered soundlessly over flowering shrubs and fern that had sprung up in pockets of soil on the stony mountainside.

The acolytes had dismounted and had moved off to look down the valley below the ledge-like path at bamboos in the shade, tossing feathery heads in rhythm with the wind, and the unsheathed balisier flowers on the slope.

The priest was alone with Benn.

'Are you very drunk?' he asked.

A picoplat was whistling on the bough of a near-by hog-plum tree, and in the air was the smell of hog-plum, and the acrid scent of the faeces the donkeys had plopped like spongecakes on the track.

'Tired, priest. I am a tired man.'

'You have become tired rather suddenly,' the priest said, looking down at the spread-out figure of Benn.

Benn sat up, and looked suspiciously at Father Vincent.

'Priest, you want to know about me. You want to save me. Can you save me, Father?'

'What makes you think I want to know about you?'

'It is the way of priests. They want to know about you. They want to do good. Save you from hell.'

Father Vincent didn't say anything, and Benn leaned back on his elbows.

'Anytime I think about things, I get tired and sick. I do not feel to work. Do not feel it make sense to go on ... Then I get drunk, and even then, priest ... even then, I have a suspicion that it doesn't matter if I go on or don't go on ... It doesn't matter.'

'It does matter,' Father Vincent said softly.

Benn's tone was half mocking.

'Today I taking you to Kumaca, and I have charge of the donkeys, so it does matter to you, priest. Tomorrow you are back in your house at Zanilla, it does not matter anymore.'

'It does matter.'

A pained smile broke over Benn's face. He nodded his head many times.

'You are right, priest. It does matter. To the donkeys it does matter. If I do not go, they get a rest. You are very right, priest.'

Benn sat now with knees drawn up, his chin resting upon them. The priest, who had been standing, now sat down beside him on the bare ground. He spoke in a kindly voice.

'How did you spend Christmas, Benn?'

Benn turned slowly, suspiciously, fixed his red-rimmed eyes upon Father Vincent.

'Why you want to know that for? You want to know about me, priest. You want to know about me!'

'Do you earnestly think so?' the priest asked.

'They always want to know about you,' Benn said in a sad, slurring tone. 'At the tennis club where I work picking up the ball and sweeping, they want to know. And Captain Grant, he want to know

60

... Work for Captain Grant nine years ... Ah! Tell you about Captain Grant, priest?'

'Do you want to?' Father Vincent asked him.

Benn looked at the hills. He shook his head. He got to his feet, looked down at the priest.

'Nine years I work for Captain Grant. Was young that time, strong and handsome. Clean out the stables, see 'bout the horses, see 'bout the cows too ... And Capt'n Grant ... Shoulda kill that man, priest ... And Capt'n Grant had plenty horses. And one o' the horses had a foal. Foal didn't look good, look sick, like it going to die. Capt'n Grant see the foal and he say, "Benn, this foal ain't no good." "Give it to me, Capt'n," I say in a joke. And now he say, "This is a good little horse, Benn. Can't give away my stock like that." "Awright, Capt'n," I say. "But I'll sell it for five pounds," the Captain sez. "Wanto buy it?" "Don't have five pounds, chief. But if you take it outa my pay, yes, I'll buy it." And you know why I'd buy it, priest? Was because when I ask about it, it come important.

'So I buy the little horse and carry it home ... Shoulda kill Captain Grant, priest ... Carry the horse home. Priest, it was a little spider-leggedy thing, and when my wife see it, she say, "Five pounds!" and she put she face so ...'

Benn stretched his mouth, and cut his eyes to show what he meant.

'And, Father, I mind that little horse like it's a child. True I thief little bit o' Captain Grant oats and some o' his medicine, but was no more than anybody used to thief. The li'l horse grow, and it was pretty, priest. Was pretty and black and shiny and smart and quick. Was so pretty, priest, didn't want anybody to see it ... Maybe I shoulda keep it home, it was so smart. But I had pay five pounds for it. It was my own. I owned it. So one day I decide to ride it to work. Had no fancy bridle and thing, but I ride it to work. And tell the truth, I feel proud sitting on my horse. Feel like the whole world fit inside my chest, and I could take two more worlds in there was how big I feel, priest. And I ride the horse to work. And Captain Grant stand up and watch me riding to work on the horse. And I see how he stand up, and I see the way he watching me and the horse, and I know that he know how big I feel inside me.

'"Mornin', Capt'n Grant," I say. And he stand up watching the horse and he say, "Mornin'. Fine horse you have there." "It all right," I say. "Yes-s," he sez. "Fine horse. Wanto sell it?" "Can't sell this horse, Captain," I say in my mind. Because you know, priest, a man is a man. Ain't a man a man, priest?'

'Yes,' the priest said.

'Well, Father, a man ain't a man ... But that time I thinking that a man is a man. So I say, "Horse not for sale, Captain." And I feeling frighten already because Captain Grant is a man like that. He wants something, he going to get it. But this horse is mine. Is mine. Not this horse, I say inside me.

'"How much you'll take for it?" he ask. "Ain't enough money in this parta the world to pay for this horse," I say, like I heard same Captain tell Mr Rivers, another white man, one time when they was talking about a bull Captain Grant had. Captain smile now and he walk away. I get off the horse and pat it on the neck, tie it up and go to work.

'Evening now, I going home. Captain Grant right there standing up by the horse. "I will give you twenty pounds for the horse," he sez, and he serious. Now, I real frighten. I say, "Captain, is the one only single horse I have. I really don't want to sell." And this time I like a little field nigger moaning and crying and whimpering. "I'll give you another horse in exchange, and fifteen pounds," sez Capt'n Grant. And now I hear the tone o' the man voice that he mean what he say. And I know if I want to find work tomorrow I better sell him the horse I only pay five pounds for and mind with his own oats and medicine besides. But inside me I cry, A man is a man. And Captain Grant standing there watching me and watching the horse. Then just so I stay there and realize that Captain Grant is a bad man. He is bad because he have fifty horses of his own, and I have one, but this one too pretty for me. And inside me I feel big still, though I frighten. I feel bigger than ten Captain Grant. But I have to work, have wife and children to feed. But I know I'm a man too, and I see the captain watching me. And now I sez, just like am a white man myself, and have fifty horses, and have riding breeches, and leather whip ... I sez, "Captain Grant, you like the horse?" "It's a fine handsome animal." "Well, I can't sell it, Captain. But if you like it, I give it to you. Take it." And priest, I stand up there and watch the Captain face turn all colours, and he strike his boots with his leather whip, and he watch me. "I give you the horse, Captain Grant," I say, and I want to cry, and feel all the pain, priest and the greatness of Jesus Christ on the Cross when they nailing him with nails and he forgiving them. I take my little bag that I carry breakfast to work in, and I turn to walk home. Captain Grant say, "Benn, you can't do this. I have to pay you for the animal." And no. I wouldn't accept a cent, priest. Captain argued, and he wanted the horse and he wanted to pay me. No, priest. No payment, and I didn't want any other horse, nor fifteen other horses. Went home, walked. And my wife had no sugar in the house, and I tell her the story, and not a word – she didn't say a word, priest. She understand how it was with the horse.

'Next day, Captain Grant shoot the horse, priest. He *shoot the horse* . . . say it break a leg. Break what leg? Shoot the horse because I wouldn't let him pay for it. I take out my poniard to cut that man to pieces. They hold me down. I bawl. I cry. They hold me down. I was going to kill him, priest. And I shoulda kill him. And if I didn't leave the work, I'd have killed him. You want to know about me, priest, well, I tell you about me . . . Why did he have to shoot the horse for, priest?'

The priest sat saying nothing for a while.

'Are you quite sure that it didn't break a leg?' he asked Benn.

'Break what leg, priest? The man shoot my horse *because* I wouldn't let him pay me for it. And he was too big not to pay for it. It didn't worth him nutten' anymore because he wasn't depriving me of it anymore because he couldn't buy it. He shoot the horse. He shoot *me*, priest . . . Eh, you don't understand, eh, Father?' Benn asked, leaning and looking down at the priest.

Father Vincent stood up.

'I understand how you felt. But maybe the horse did break a leg.'

'Excuse me, priest, but you take me for a fool too. Come. I am not so tired now. We will travel to Kumaca.'

The journey continued in a long, tense silence. Father Vincent rode just behind Benn. Then they had to dismount and walk where the path was very narrow. They crossed the narrow part. The priest offered Benn a cigarette. Benn looked at it, then took it. He waved away the offer of a light. He would smoke it later.

'Do you think it would rain?' Father Vincent asked. He had seen a cloud in the sky, but his real object was to make conversation.

'It is only a passing cloud. It will not rain,' Benn said.

'We are lucky to have such good weather at this time of year.'

'Yes,' Benn said.

'Even for Christmas we were lucky,' the priest said.

They mounted the animals again. The priest rode very near to Benn.

'You did not tell me how you spent Christmas.'

'I will tell you,' Benn said, the edge of aggression in his tone.

They had ridden a further quarter of a mile in silence. Benn spoke: 'I will tell you, priest. It doesn't make sense a man like me going on. I look at the New Year coming in, and I think, Where am I going? Where am I going, priest? After Captain Grant murdered my horse, I do not have anything. My horse is dead.'

'And before the horse, what did you have?' the priest asked.

'I was young. I was strong. I was handsome. I had no need for anything. But I tell you about Christmas. For Christmas, I buy a toy for the children. I buy a little train in the store at Zanilla for my littlest son. I myself play with it. You turn it like the chain of a clock, then it runs. I buy some balloons also. My wife say to me that I waste the money. I do not think I waste the money, priest. I say to the woman, I give you money to buy things for the house, and I myself buy rum for when the neighbours come over, and when the paran pass playing the quatros and singing the seranales for Christmas. But I am glad I buy this one train. And you vex for that? She thinks that they need shoes. They need shirts, and pants, and dress. They need books to go to school . . . I buy a train for the littlest one. She says if I cannot buy for all, I should not buy for one. But he is five years old! And I like the train. Nobody ever buy a train for me, and I buy one for my little boy. Priest, a man must buy something for his little son. It is very important. And if I wait to say that I do not have the money to buy for all of them, I will never buy anything for anyone.'

'How many children do you have?' Father Vincent asked.

Benn held up both hands, opened them to show the stubby fingers. He turned down the thumb of one hand.

'Many,' the priest said.

'What else for a man to do? Maybe one of them come out something.'

'And still you can afford to get drunk?' the priest asked incredulously.

'It is for that I get drunk. I have to afford to get drunk, priest. For my own self inside me I must get drunk. For Christmas I go out with the paran and sing and they give me the quatro to play sometimes, but I do not get drunk. I look at the people. Always at Christmas I look at the people and do not get drunk.'

'And why did you drink to get drunk today?'

'I tell you, it is necessary . . . I try to understand something, try to see something, priest.'

'I do not understand what you can see when you get drunk?' the priest asked with perhaps too much gravity, as if the question itself were not ridiculous.

'You do not understand. I try to see if it makes sense even getting drunk. Priest, a man must do something for himself. Even if it is to get drunk. For me, for myself I get drunk. Otherwise it is no sense coming over these hills. If I cannot even get drunk! I cannot buy dress for my wife. I cannot buy toys for all my children. And I cannot get drunk? You understand, priest?'

'But, Benn, you have the responsibilities of a family.'

'You do not understand. Listen, priest. I have these responsibilities, yes. But I must be something, somehow. I must – I must – ' Ben searched for the word he wanted – 'I must know myself, feel myself . . . No, I do not make myself clear. You do not understand, and I cannot explain. Listen, priest. I must be me in order to think of my family. Otherwise it is nothing at all. Just only coming over these hills and giving the money I make to my wife. I cannot be like a hen who lays the eggs only for the farmer, or like these donkeys that go over the hills at my command.

'And tell you something, priest. I am afraid not to want to get drunk. Because it would mean that I give up, that I surrender to be nothing. I have to get drunk. But sometimes I get drunk and still I ask, what is this? What does it mean? You are still nothing! But way inside me, I say, Benn, you are drunk and you do not know what you are saying. But, priest, to stay sober and see that it is nothing, to realize that I am nothing. Ah! It is hard-hard.'

Benn's face was creased and showed excitement.

'Priest, I refuse to be a donkey. Is a man a donkey, priest?'

Father Vincent said, 'A man has an immortal soul.'

Benn repeated: 'A man has an immortal soul . . . I have an immortal soul.'

'And what does Mrs Benn say to all this . . . this getting drunk?'

'Like you, priest, she doesn't understand. She understand about the horse, but this she doesn't understand. Maybe it is how she is getting old, and has surrendered. She say, Benn, you get drunk again? She say, Benn, I going to have to leave you. I know, poor thing, she will not leave me. She say, think about the children, Benn. Oh, God, I try to make her understand that it is because of the children I must get drunk. Ah, Father! she say plenty, that woman. And sometime I sober and home in the little house, or out in the back where we make a little garden, and the sweat run down my face, and I see my children running half-naked and I scream, Father, in my mind I scream. I know I am dying, I know it is no use. I am dead, priest. I am nothing! A donkey! I have a soul, Father! I cannot die? . . . So I get drunk and tell that to me, because sober I can say nothing, only scream. Yes, I am sorry to spend the money in the rumshop when in the house the money could buy bread and sugar. And cannot remember when last my wife buy a dress for herself. I am sorry. But it is necessary for me to get drunk, priest. I do not know me. I do not know where I am going. But you know who you are, priest. You know that you are the priest in the white gown from . . . Where are you from priest?'

Father Vincent said, 'I come from Ireland.'

'It is near to England, eh?'

'It is.'

'What kind of place it is?'

'It is a strange country to talk about. It is lovely, and lonely, and talkative. Really, I do not know how to talk to you about Ireland.'

Benn said, 'From Ireland, the priest in his white gown. And you know where you are going when you die, and have never had in your heart thoughts to kill a man. And you want to save people. Ah!'

'You drink too much and too often, Benn,' the priest said.

'You said you'd pray for me. And still I get drunk as before.' Benn said, smiling now.

'You must make yourself strong for your temptations, then,' the priest said.

'For me, to get drunk is necessary, priest. It is very necessary.'

Journeying. The priest and Benn not speaking, only the acolytes behind them jabbering in whispers. Birds whistling. The sound of wind through the cool forest.

'We will be in time, priest,' Benn said.

Father Vincent had been looking at his watch.

'And now that there is a house for the schoolmaster, you could sleep if you care to. The sunshine is pretty in the morning here, and the birds are all singing. You will like that, Father,' Benn said.

'I will like it, yes. But I will like it better to get back tonight.'

'You will get back.'

'Tell me, have you met the schoolmaster?' Father Vincent asked.

'I see him plenty times.'

The priest did not say anything.

'Always in his tie and jacket,' Benn said.

'You do not like him, Benn,' the priest said.

'I do not say that at all.'

'There was something in your voice,' said the priest.

'I do not have anything against the man. They all like him in Kumaca. Everything he is in it. Everything. Sometimes I think they even want him to take these donkeys over the hills.'

'Oh, he is very popular. It is good.'

'He is popular, priest. He writes letters for the people. He is doing great work in the village, and is organizing things. He organize the village council and the singing choir. And he write to the government to build a well for the people to get water. And since he is there now, there is always talk of the building of a road through from Valencia. He write many letters about it already.'

'Good,' the priest said. 'And in the school? The children?'

'The children go to the school and they learn to read and to write.'

'But still you are not very enthusiastic over him. You are a cautious man.'

'Look at the grey hairs in my head, priest. And always I think of that Captain Grant, and my horse that he shoot.'

'But this schoolmaster is your own. Your own people.'

'He is black, yes. But not my own people. Priest, he is closer to your people. I think he is your people. He learned in your schools, and he wears the clothes the way you wear them, and he talks the way you talk, and his thinking is that of your people. He is yours, priest. He is not mine.'

'But he had to learn somewhere,' Father Vincent said.

'I do not say no, priest. But you say he is our people, when he is yours. I know he had to learn somewhere.'

Father Vincent said, 'Benn, you are a difficult man.'

'Father, I had a beautiful black horse. He shoot the horse. Out of spite, he shoot the horse. I shoulda kill Captain Grant ... But for that, they hang people.'

When the party rode into Kumaca, they found the place deserted. Father Vincent, who had fixed his adjustable smile on his face in preparation for returning the glad, pious salutations of the villagers, felt silly wearing a grin that threatened to serve no purpose except to make him feel foolish and fraudulent.

'What is this?' he asked helplessly.

He missed those village girls with their wide eyes and large brassièreless chests, and the toothless smiles of the old women and the grave bowing of the men.

Benn did not know what was wrong.

'Maybe they are sick,' one of the bright acolytes ventured.

Benn looked back at him, and shook his head.

In this unreal and unfamiliar silence, the small group made its way to the schoolhouse.

At the schoolhouse, Father Vincent could only sit on his ass and gape. There lined in two rows were the villagers, big and small; men and women, wearing fixed smiles on their faces that reminded the priest, with a touch of guilt and pain, of his own mechanical smile. At the head of the lines, at the door of the open schoolhouse proud and grand in grey suit, polka-dot bow-tie, grey felt hat, rimless spectacles, his face serious, and stance military, stood the schoolmaster. Father Vincent, before he could get over his surprise and come to himself, saw the schoolmaster lift his hands, gesturing like the conductor of the London Philharmonic, noticed that there was a switch in his right hand, saw the switch go up with a sharp, rather precise, yet overbearingly dramatic and somehow graceful movement, heard the first notes of the hymn, 'Come, Holy Ghost' burst upon his ears.

Caught, embarrassed, Father Vincent tried not to look at the schoolmaster. Instead he selected for his gaze of forced approval, the pink throat of a robust woman whose efforts to drown out the other members of the choir increased immediately she became aware of this special attention. Concerned about the over-all harmony, and very concerned about the robust woman's voice box, the priest, without a change in expression, turned from the woman's beaming face and in his mind guided the hymn anxiously to its conclusion. However, before he could collect himself and dismount, Mr Warrick's baton was trembling in the air above his stern forehead, and the priest realized that he would have to sit through maybe the 'Ave Maria'. It was 'O Holy Night'. He tried to disregard the pink throat of the buxom lady, but hearing her screeching furiously, and suspecting, rather, knowing that she was expecting – no, demanding his attention once more, he turned in her direction, and smiled, before fixing his eyes on the schoolmaster who conducted the choir to the end of the song. And not wanting to be caught once more, and seriously believing that it was not beyond the schoolmaster to subject him to another hymn, he cleared his throat in the large, nervous, expectant silence, and said, 'Good day, good day. God bless you. God bless you,' bowed lightly, smiled his hypocritical smile, and began to get off the donkey that was beginning to bray its applause now. And as his feet touched ground, the schoolmaster was at his side, bowing now, showing his teeth, and asking with his entire countenance how did he like the performance. Father Vincent, in the voice in which he uttered amens, muttered, 'Fine, Mr Warrick. Fine. Fine.'

'Come this way, please, Father. I have a place prepared for you,' the schoolmaster said.

And if he had not been priest, and Mr Warrick not schoolmaster of Kumaca RC, he would have surely remarked, 'If it were not so, I would not have told you.' Instead, he said, 'Very well, Mr Warrick. What about my acolytes?'

'I will have them attended to, Father.'

The priest followed the schoolmaster to the house where he washed up and prepared for the mass. Then with the acolytes, he went across to the schoolhouse where the congregation had already gathered. After the mass, the priest was ready to leave. He had deliberately put off speaking to the schoolmaster until he was able to observe him, and to see the reactions of the villagers to him.

But now it was time to leave, and he was on the front gallery of the schoolmaster's house.

'How has it been going, Mr Warrick?'

'I think very good, Father. We have a series of activities in the village now. The people are very keen. Very keen.'

'That is good. And how are the children progressing at school?'

'They are coming along fine, Father. Of course we have a few who are quite hopeless, but by and large, they are doing quite well.'

'And the adults?'

'Not many of them attend day school, but we have been able to arrange something in the village council, and now many of them can sign their names.'

'Maybe we have time for a quick look at the school,' Father Vincent suggested.

The schoolmaster looked at the watch on his wrist.

'We will have to be quick, Father.'

'Let's go. Tell me, how is Miss Dandrade getting on? Is she much help?'

'She is a fine young lady, Father. Her work is quite good.'

'We will have to pay her, Mr Warrick.'

The schoolmaster hesitated.

'Don't you think she should be paid?'

'By all means, Father. By all means. Her work is quite good.'

They walked through the school.

'The benches seem to have held up quite well,' the priest said.

'We are very strict with them, Father. We are strict with the care of all furniture. And the village council assists with any repairs we need to make.'

'This village council of yours seems quite active, Mr Warrick.'

'It is, Father. We are hoping that our representations to government for a road in from Valencia would meet with approval. In fact, we are quite certain that they will. There is so much in this village. You have cocoa and ground provisions, yams, and bananas. If there is a road to transport the produce out of here, it will do wonders for the economy of the place. Then we are also quite rich in timber.'

'What about gold, Mr Warrick?'

The schoolmaster smiled.

'Yes,' Father Vincent said. 'Things seem to be going quite well. Keep up the good work, Mr Warrick.'

'I will continue to do my best, Father.'

'Yes, yes yes,' the priest said vaguely, thinking now that it was time to be starting back to Valencia.

'Well, I must be leaving now, schoolmaster.'

'I wish you a pleasant trip back, Father.'

'Good evening, Mr Warrick.'

'Good evening, Father.'

Chapter Six

I

Ignacio Dardain had closed the doors of his shop for the night, and now, under the light of the gas lamp, he stood behind the counter, looking over his accounts. Now and again he would remove the pencil from behind his ear and add a figure here and a figure there, slowly, carefully.

Easter had come now, and gone; but because of the lateness of the cocoa crop this year, many of the accounts had remained unpaid. It was to these that he was adding, by changing a figure here and a figure there, his interest. He was not robbing anybody. A man had to know how to live. The shop could not run on goodwill. In the shops of Zanilla there were many clever signs. 'Trust dead, Credit kill him', was one of them. But he had his own system. He had his way of dealing with delinquent accounts. In fact he did not care too much if some of the accounts mounted. The people of Kumaca who had accounts at his shop, all owned lands. If they could not pay in cash . . . well . . . there was always the matter of an agreement. He himself sold the stamps.

Looking over the accounts now, Dardain remembered that his own stock was short after the Easter holiday, and that he would have to make a journey to Zanilla soon to build back his stock. In Zanilla too he had to fill an order for Consantine Patron who wanted some materials for the extension he was making to his house. He could not understand Consantine Patron at all. He had been one of the men always in the lead in the affairs of the village, but, since the death of Lucien and the coming of the schoolmaster he had withdrawn gradually and finally from the affairs of the village, and looked on now in a sort of sneering, pompous silence, and even for Easter, although the schoolmaster had invited him to make a speech at the opening of the big Easter celebrations, he had not remained at Kumaca, but went to Valencia to fight his cocks in the gayelle there where, they say, he won many battles. He said that it was all foolishness this giving of speeches at the Easter celebrations and that

72

all these new things the schoolmaster was introducing would only spoil the fun that the people were accustomed to having at their fête. He was jealous of the popularity of the schoolmaster, that was it. But he was very foolish. The schoolmaster was a new man, and intelligent, so the people listened to him. Paulaine Dandrade worked in a different way. He was prepared to listen to what the schoolmaster had to say, and to support him if necessary. Whenever he had an objection to make, he made it. Nothing was taken away from him in the eyes of the villagers; and the schoolmaster did not lose respect for him.

Like him or not, everybody had to admit that the schoolmaster was a worker. And if he liked to show off a bit, what was that? He had the learning, and knew how to speak, and wore his clothes well. And the people accepted him as he was. Already he had done much for the village, and soon, maybe in August, because of the letters he had written to government, they would begin building the road in from Valencia. That would be the best thing to happen to Kumaca. That would be the best thing to happen to Dardain himself, because he now owned almost all the lands along which the road must pass. Also with the expected increase in trade, more money would circulate, and his shop would do much more business. Dardain liked the schoolmaster very much. It was only fair; for after all, how could a man help but like the person who would be responsible for making him the richest man in Kumaca. But such a man, thought Dardain, you should also be a little afraid of. Too much depended upon him. However, let him cause the road to be built; when that is done, we shall see.

Removing the pencil from behind his ear, Dardain made another change on an account. When he sold his lands to government, perhaps he would not need to add so much interest.

Trust dead. Credit kill him. The slogan tumbled over in his brain, and Dardain's lean, sharp face took on what really was for him a smile, a sinking of the hollow cheeks, a twitching of the nose, and an accompanying low, strangling sound from closed lips.

Now there was a knock on the door. Dardain reached for the torchlight which he always kept close at hand. He went to the window which was already half opened, pushed it, shone the torchlight outside to see who was the person wanting to make this late purchase.

It was the son of Landeau, who lived near to the school.

'What you want now?'

After closing hours, Dardain always adopted a tough way of speaking, as if at such a time merely putting up the price of the commodity was not sufficient compensation for the disturbance of his peace.

'I bring a message from the schoolmaster, Mr Dardain. He say for you to come over now. It is important.'

'Wonder what he want to see me for now,' he grumbled, still talking tough, although he knew quite well that he would go.

'All right. Tell him I coming in a while.'

Dardain withdrew the torchlight and shut the window.

He thought: Ah, so at last he send to call me, eh. Good . . . Good!

But in fact, Dardain was not happy. He had, over the past few years, managed to acquire almost all the lands through which the track passed and along which the road to Kumaca was expected to be built, with the hope of selling it to government at a good profit. He had been very patient and very ingenious, but although he had receipts for the purchases he had made, for one reason or another, not all the land titles had been transferred to his name.

Now that the possibilities of the road seemed excellent, some of those villagers from whom he had acquired lands suddenly realized that they might have released their lands at too cheap a price, and had (he understood – he usually knew everything that went on in Kumaca anyway) gone quietly to the schoolmaster for him to advise them, and perhaps seek recompense on their behalf. As with a certain class of people with little knowledge in these things, not only did those who still retained the titles in name go but others who had no claim whatsoever had gone and appealed to the schoolmaster. The schoolmaster was always talking about the upliftment of the downtrodden masses, and it would not surprise Dardain if he decided to take up the matter on behalf of the people concerned. On the other hand, Dardain, always conscious of his investment and of the role of the schoolmaster both as a power in the village and in the building of the road, had carefully seen to it that he gave no offence whatever to him. At meetings of the village council, whatever the schoolmaster said was, for Dardain, law. For the sports at Easter this year, he had given more prizes than he had ever given before. Perhaps the only area in which he might have caused slight offence was that he occasionally offered the schoolmaster a bottle of whisky which the schoolmaster studiously refused on one or another pretext. This fact made Dardain concerned. The schoolmaster might be a very difficult man to deal with when the time came.

Better carry a bottle of whisky for him, Dardain thought, when he was ready to leave.

He shone the torchlight on the shelves.

No. I will not carry it. He is not that kind. I must be very careful. Although I have nothing to fear, because it was all done legal and with stamps on every agreement that I make with the people. No, I will not carry it.

But outside, moving away from the shop, Dardain felt uncomfortable; he felt that he needed a prop. He should have taken the whisky with him. However, it was too late for that. To turn back was bad luck.

There was a light in the house of the schoolmaster. Dardain went up the path, and knocked on the door.

'That you, Mr Dardain? Come in.'

'Good night, schoolmaster,' Dardain said in his brisk, patronizing manner.

He had opened the door and entered the room which by Kumaca's standards was quite spacious. It was sparsely furnished and clean. The schoolmaster sat at a table, with books scattered all about him. He did not rise. He looked over his spectacles and motioned Dardain to a chair.

'Sorry to disturb you at this hour, Mr Dardain. But you can see that I also am busy working.'

'It is no trouble, schoolmaster,' Dardain said, thinking: It is in his face. We must talk.

'I wanted to talk to you about the road which we have been struggling so long and so hard for. As you know – or, do you know?'

'What, schoolmaster?'

'We are likely to get the road very soon. The surveyors should be ready to begin mapping.'

Dardain hid his delight. He waited.

'It is very good news, schoolmaster. We must congratulate you.'

The schoolmaster smiled.

'Thank you. But don't congratulate me too quickly. There are some matters which must be dealt with before the road becomes a reality. That's why I asked to see you.'

'You know I am always willing to help, schoolmaster.'

The schoolmaster picked up his pen and began to doodle upon the piece of paper before him.

'There is a problem,' he said, looking over his spectacles at Dardain.

In setting the stage for a deal, you had to make talking an easy matter.

Dardain said, 'A problem, schoolmaster?'

'Yes. As you know, we were all the time pressing for the road to pass along the existing track. Suddenly I find that there is a great deal of confusion about ownership of the lands concerned. It seems that ownership has been changing steadily over the past six, seven years . . .'

'And where is the problem, schoolmaster?'

'Well, people complain. They do not seem to be quite certain. You own some of those lands. I guess you would know about this confusion of land titles.'

'Every agreement I make with people I do fair and legal and with stamps, schoolmaster.'

'It is a very complex situation, Mr Dardain,' the schoolmaster said, looking at Dardain, inviting him to comment.

'Schoolmaster, I am a poor man trying my best with a little shop and much worries. I try to enterprise. I do much work for the people before you come. I sell my goods in the shop, and they sometimes cannot pay. I wait. I am a businessman. They still cannot pay. My goods cost money. So they say, you better take piece of land. So we do business with the land. A little portion here, a little portion there. It is not good to have land scattered all about, so I make sacrifice, and buy the pieces between. So I own the lands now. I do not rob anybody. It is a business.'

'I do not like how the people complain, Mr Dardain. Assume that the government as a result of their complaints decide to investigate.'

Dardain cut him short.

'They can investigate, Mr Schoolmaster. I have nothing to hide.'

76

'But during the investigation, there will be no work on the road. You see, the progress of the road can be held back because of this confusion. I do not like it. Perhaps it might be better to go back to the suggestion made by the preliminary survey team. You remember they advised that because of the landslide it might have been better to cut the road along another path. It was only after I had made my recommendation they decided that the present path would do quite well.'

Dardain's voice came out thick and strained.

'You cannot do that, schoolmaster. You cannot.'

The schoolmaster linked the fingers of both his hands, and rested his elbows on the table. He looked steadily at Dardain.

'I agree it would cost more, and would involve more time, but perhaps that is the best way out.'

Dardain realized now that he had slipped. He must be careful. There must be no more outbursts. He had been a businessman too long a time not to know that deals were not made by emotional outbrusts.

In his most humble tone, Dardain said, 'The present track is the best for the road. There is no big forest to cut down, and to get away from the landslide, all they have to do is to go a little higher where the land is firm.'

Dardain paused. He said, 'That talk about another path was just an excuse to put off building the road until perhaps another ten, twenty years.'

It was like a game of draughts, making a deal, Dardain thought. First, you push a knob, then you sit back and look at the board, watched where the other fellow pushed.

'I think you have a point there, Mr Dardain. But there still remains the complaints of these people.'

'Mr Schoolmaster, you have experience. You know people. They sell me the lands, and now they see an opportunity to make something more, they go to you and complain. But they have no claim. I do it all legal and with stamps,' Dardain said, becoming more aggressive – but not as yet too aggressive.

'Let us suppose that they decide to take court action, Mr Dardain? What happens? The entire project comes to a halt until the action is settled. And you know these matters drag on sometimes for years in the courts. And meanwhile, the poor people of Kumaca are suffering for lack of a road, and all the work – the good work we have done – goes to nought.'

'I do it all legal and with stamps. The people have no claim,' Dardain said doggedly.

'Yet they can take you to the courts. Or for that matter, they can claim the lands themselves, then you will have to take them to court to prove that the lands are really yours. Waste of time, waste of money. If some settlement cannot be arrived at, it is better that we abandon the idea of the present track entirely.'

'You are a hard man, schoolmaster.'

'No, Mr Dardain. I try to think of what is beneficial to the community as a whole. That is all.'

'You are a hard man, schoolmaster,' Dardain said again, inflecting his voice with a feeling of admiration.

Dardain scratched his head, leaned forward in his chair.

'Schoolmaster, let us talk reasonable,' he said.

'We have been talking, Mr Dardain.'

'As man to man, let us talk now.'

'Mr Dardain,' the schoolmaster said, 'I hope you are not asking me to use my influence to prevent the people taking action against you. Although perhaps as you put it they might not have very much of a case. Yet . . . yet we must think of what is best for Kumaca.'

'But yes, Mr Schoolmaster. But yes!'

'Schoolmaster, you are a man of intelligence. I been to all parts of this country, and I meet people, and I know an intelligent man when I see him, and a man with the good of the people at heart. Try a cigarette?' Dardain asked, removing his pack and offering one to the schoolmaster.

'No, thanks.'

Dardain lit his cigarette, and leaned back in the chair.

'Schoolmaster, this is not a matter that cannot be settled. How many times I see you in this very village, and I right by your side giving you support in the things you do, eh? And for the Easter look how you bring order into the fête that was a big bacchanal, and make people realize that you must have order in your affairs. Look how you get the children to learn to read, and the big people can sign their name now. And the village council you bring together to solve the problems and to give the village weight when we talk to the government official. And today, you are the man in Kumaca, schoolmaster. You can make and you can break. So now there is this matter of the road which nobody ever work hard for as you. And you know if we do not get the road now we will not get it for next ten maybe twenty years. The people complain to you. I do not believe that the problem too big to solve.'

Dardain watched the schoolmaster playing now with the handle of his pen.

'Schoolmaster, you say you are a reasonable man. I say I am a reasonable man. Tell me, cannot two reasonable men get together and talk? Eh? You think I get the lands for nothing? Or too cheap? Do I give it back? Can I give back the lands, schoolmaster? How can I do such a thing? We are reasonable men, schoolmaster, and can solve this matter right here, tonight. What matters to me is the road. What matters to you is the road. What matters to the men who come to survey, and to the people, and to the government officials, is the road. We can settle the matter right here now. Do I talk reasonable, schoolmaster? If I do not talk with sense, then tell me, and I will leave and go home right now.'

Dardain watched the schoolmaster with his eyes lowered looking at the handle of the pen with which he was still playing absently.

'A man works, schoolmaster. I work hard. And what you have to show after a little time gone, and they forget your name. Because it is the way of people. They forget. And Christ was crucified, eh? And so a man works and there is nothing to show. But where the cow is tied, he must graze there, eh? Do I talk unreasonable? You are an intelligent man, schoolmaster. You are working very hard. And you will be forgotten. Uriah Reeves they forget, and Merryship and even Lucien who die just a few months now, they do not speak his name anymore. You think I tell you this only because I have some profit in the matter if the road comes through the place where I have the land? I tell you this, because, like me, you are a man who thinks that you will do good, and help the people. If you are wise, you must think of yourself too. Tell me. I talk without reason, schoolmaster? If I talk without sense, tell me, and I will take my torchlight and leave you to do whatever you want, and you can advise the people to take me to court if that is your mind.'

The schoolmaster put down the pen with which he had been playing, fixed his spectacles on his face. He looked at Dardain. His voice was hoarse when he spoke.

'To talk so long without a drink in this climate is not in good taste,' he said. 'What will you have?'

Holding an iron grip on his sense of release and feeling of relief now, Dardain said, 'I will take anything . . . rum will do.'

Yes, I have rum.'

The schoolmaster very properly pushed out his chair, and stood to go to get the liquor.

Much later that night, when the rum had slid half-way down the bottle, Dardain finally took leave of the schoolmaster. And, walking home behind the beam of his flashlight, he would stop to look up at the heavens and the many stars, stop to feel too the cool, fine night. He had nothing to fear now. He had been a businessman too long not to know that one hand by itself couldn't clap. The schoolmaster had been a hard one. But one had to pay. One had to pay a price for everything. As a businessman, this was too elementary a consideration to deserve discussion.

Chapter Seven

I

Time goes slowly in Kumaca, and events are significant. People are concerned about a baby being born, an old woman dying, and the friendship that two old men, who are very often arguing, have for each other. They are aware of these things and are not puzzled by them. And they know who is repairing his house, and who is sick. They take time out to look at a boy and a girl who are very shy with each other, and very much in love. They watch developments and wait. They have experience in these things, and in many intricate ways, share in them. But there are other things which they notice as well, things that hold their interest for the moment because they are unfamiliar – they are suspicious of the unfamiliar. They see now that the schoolmaster has bought a beautiful, white horse. They stand at the roadside and watch him ride past on its back, and they wave or say good morning and comment among themselves They notice also that now Dardain is very often at the house of the schoolmaster, and the schoolmaster at Dardain's place. They watch these things and do not dwell too long on them, because there is a girl walking out for the first time her first baby, and if you look at the child, you must put a bit of silver in its hand; and there is an old man burying his wife, he is very sad and the tears dry up in his eyes and do not fall; and a boy and girl whom they have known as infants walk always the one with the other: all these hard, beautiful things claim them. They knew where some things will lead, and why some things are; but about the visits between Dardain and the schoolmaster, and of the schoolmaster's white horse, they do not know. They do not have much experience in these things. They do not know where they will lead.

II

From the clearing near the balata tree high in the forest of Kumaca, Pedro Assivero could see the sun setting in Maracas over Chupara

Bay. And when he turned from the sight, it was already getting dark, and birds were screaming and flapping about as they sought nests before the last sunlight left the land. Pedro yawned and stretched, all in one action, like a cat, then he bent and picked up the writing-pad in which he had placed the fine sheet of pale blue paper with a pattern worked in gold around the edges. He had spoiled the other sheet, and had written on more than half the pages of the writing-pad before he had it done as he wanted it, with the handwriting good, and the words with the proper spelling, and the words giving the feeling that he wanted them to give. Now he took up the bottle of ink, and began to walk. He was very anxious now, and wished that he could just wish it and be home; yet, he did not run, and although he had his flute in his pocket, he did not think of playing it. He was very serious now, and tonight he would have to talk to his father.

Pedro reached home, and went into the room which he shared with his smaller brother, Robert, who had been ill now for eight months, and who could barely walk, and did not, could not, go to school, although it was his burning desire to do so. He was very close to this brother, and liked to talk with him, because he was a fine gentle boy who was also smart and could feel things, and said many fine things and asked questions of intelligence, and could read now, because whatever Pedro learned at school, he came home and showed it to Robert and went over the things in a book, so that Robert who had only fourteen years could read, perhaps better than Pedro himself.

Robert was reading by the light of a kerosene lamp, and he looked up from the book when Pedro came into the room. He was very sensitive, and at a glance could see that there was something unusual in Pedro's face.

'What is it, Pedro?'

Pedro sat on the edge of the bed.

'It is nothing. I am tired. I was all the time in the forest writing.'

Pedro broke off.

'. . . Robert, why do you read by this light? It will spoil your eyes, the schoolmaster says. A candle is better.'

'Mama put the light in the room, and I use it. But as you say, brother, I will get a candle.'

'I will get one for you in a little while. You must take care of your eyes.'

Robert raised himself by his elbows, and now rested his back on the wooden bed's head.

'How is it with you, Pedro? There is something in your face.'

You are too keen, Robert. I am very anxious. I have to talk to Papa tonight.'

'He is over at the house of Consantine Patron. I hear they go again to Valencia with the fighting cocks, at the end of next week. What makes you anxious so?'

Pedro lifted the hand which held the writing-pad between whose leaves he had the fine gold-edged sheet of paper. He hesitated, then he said:

'I have done it, Robert. I have written the letter.'

'Ah!' Robert said, his face lighting up. 'But you did not tell me. Now I know why you have that look in your face.'

Pedro said gravely, 'I will show it to you, but your hands must be clean. Do not soil it. Let me see your hands.'

'They are clean, Pedro, I do no work. I lie on this bed here, and sometimes I go and sit by the window, or before the door. My hands are very clean.'

'There is no soot from the lamp?'

'I do not touch the lamp. Your letter is very important, I will not soil it, Pedro.'

Pedro's face was very serious. He removed the sheet of paper with the writing on it. He looked at the paper, and he looked at his brother reclining on the bed.

'I do not know if you can read it.'

The smaller brother looked at the letter which Pedro still held in his hand.

'The paper is very fine, Pedro.'

'It is the best paper I could get in Kumaca. Here, read it and let me hear how it sounds. And tell me if the writing is not very good. I took painful time writing it in the forest.'

Pedro handed the sheet of paper very solemnly over to his brother who took it as if it were something very precious.

83

'The writing is very good, Pedro. You make your letters very neat,' Robert said.

'Read it.'

> 'Mr Paulaine Dandrade,
>   Kumaca.

> 'My dear Sir,
>   With much respect I take my pen in writing you this letter to ask for the hand of your daughter, Christiana.
>   A very long time I have been looking at Christiana, and I find her to be a very charming and pleasing young lady in all respects. I must tell you that I feel a great love in my heart for Christiana.
>   With your consent, I will be proud and will feel myself greatly honoured to have her to be my wife.
> >   I remain,
> >   With much respect and affection,
> >   Pedro Assivero.'

After a while of silence in which the two brothers had their eyes on the letter, Robert looked up at Pedro and spoke.

'It is a fine letter, Pedro. The words are very good. I did not know that you knew such fine words.'

'It really is a fine letter, you think, Robert, for her?'

'Really it is very fine, Pedro.'

Carefully, Pedro took the letter from his brother.

'I will show it to my father, and will ask him to carry it to Mr Paulaine for me.'

'You must ask him to let Mr Consantine go with him to see Mr Paulaine. That is the way it is done. I remember it was so when our other brother got married.'

'Robert, you remember everything. I will do as you say, and it will give more weight to my letter that such a man as Mr Consantine goes with it.'

Robert shifted on the bed.

'Brother,' he said.

'Yes, Robert.'

'You say in your letter that you have been looking at Christiana. Has she been looking at you?'

'I know it, boy. Sometimes in the school when she is teaching a class, her eyes and mine make four together, and it is like our hearts are meeting. I know it, Robert, but I cannot tell you with words how it is with Christiana and me. She knows I will write the letter.'

Pedro glanced again at the letter, then carefully put it between the covers of the writing-pad. He was very quiet.

Robert said, 'You are a man now, brother. You will have to build a house. I cannot imagine you building a house.'

'It will not be difficult for me. Papa will give me the piece of land near to the mahogany trees. And soon they start work on the road from Valencia. I will get a job and will earn some money, and will build my house before the day of the wedding. But that is yet to be arranged.'

'So you will leave school, then?'

'From today I leave, Robert. I cannot help it. I am a man now, I can write a letter now, and can read. I will buy books when I go down to Valencia. I will learn to read even better.'

'And Christiana? Will she stop teaching in the school? I hear that she is very bright, and you yourself tell me that she is taking private lessons from the schoolmaster so that she would take an examination that the other people take at Zanilla.'

'When we are married she will have things at home to do, Robert.'

'It will not be good for the school. And it will be hard for her not to take the examination after taking lessons from the schoolmaster.'

Pedro said, 'That is how things are, Robert.'

The smaller brother was silent for a while.

'Brother, if you leave school, it means that I leave school also.'

'Already you can read as well as me and you can write. If you have the books you can read for yourself. And as to the sums in the book, which you already do better than me, we will get Christiana to correct them for you. Maybe just now you get better, and go to school for yourself, maybe even take private lessons, and take the same examination like Christiana would take if she is not getting married. Eh, Robert?'

'You think I will get better, Pedro?'

'You will get better, Robert.'

Robert looked down at his feet.

'These,' he said. 'Sometimes there is no feeling at all in them. I hear the priest say it is polio. The doctors in Zanilla, he say, know nothing about that.'

'You will get better, Robert. And when I work and get money, I will ask Papa and we will take you to the big hospital in Port-of-Spain, where the doctors are many. Then who will say that you will not get better? But you will have to be able to stand the bumps on the road to Valencia.'

'I do not know if I can stand them, Pedro. Do you think they will operate? I hear they sometimes operate on people at the hospital.'

'You mean if they will have to cut off some part of your foot?'

'Will they cut it, Pedro?' the boy asked, glancing anxiously at his feet.

'I do not think so. Perhaps they have a machine to bring the muscles of your foot back in order. I will ask the schoolmaster about that.'

They were silent now and Robert opened the book that he had been reading, and closed it without reading anything.

'I will not like when you go away, Pedro. Truly.'

'I will also be sad to leave. But it is for my happiness, and for her, Robert. And you can come to where we live and spend some days and we can read books and sit down and talk about things. It will not be so bad, Robert. And we will come, Christiana and I, and look for Mama, and she will also visit us. Wait and see, Robert. It will be all right.'

'So you talk to Papa tonight?'

'I will talk with him. I will ask him to let Mr Consantine Patron go with him to the house of Mr Paulaine.'

Pedro got off the bed.

'I go now to tell Mama.'

'She also will miss you,' Robert said.

'Perhaps she will be glad to be rid of me.'

'You make a joke, Pedro. You know how she loves you. But she thinks many thoughts in her head, and says few words out of her mouth.'

86

Pedro said sadly:

'It is because of Papa. But things will not change. And they are getting old now. I am sorry to see how they are, Robert. But what can we do? I cannot stop Papa from drinking his rum. He too remembers much, and he wants to forget.'

'It is how it is, eh, Pedro?'

'Yes, Robert, it is so.'

III

Dusk now. In the muddy light, and drizzle, Christiana running home, her feet sloshing in the soft mud puddles of the track, running home in a dry, numb hysteria, through the rain, not seeing anything because of the tears filling her eyes, feeling a world of pain in her groin, her head, her belly. But she ran, her legs jogging in an awkward, mechanical rhythm, ran, whimpering and biting her bottom lip with her teeth, her face made ugly with the effort of trying to hold in the pain between her thighs, in her whole self, and restrain the tears already mixing with the raindrops on her face. Ran, stumbled against a projecting tree root across the track, fell, remained fallen, crying silently, moaning with her face against the mud, remembering now that she had fled and left her schoolbooks on the floor near the schoolmaster's bed. Vomited. Remembered and cried again, got slowly to her feet, and began to walk now, afraid.

It was still raining, and darkness was bearing down between the surrounding forest trees and the thin lines of rain. The wetness would hide her. The darkness would hide her. She was sick inside. Filthy, dead, dry, sick inside, didn't know how she would face her father. Couldn't tell him! Mustn't tell him! He would, if she told him, take up his shotgun and put a cartridge into it. Then what would happen when he killed the schoolmaster? What would happen to him, her father? No, mustn't tell him. Better to run away. Run where? Run where? Oh, God! She had not been strong at all. Had not been strong. Been not strong. Maybe it was thinking so much about Pedro, and not knowing. Not knowing, not suspecting before it was too late. Oh, she had not been strong at all. He had been too strong for her. She didn't know what happened! Didn't even know how it happened. All she could remember now was that the rain was falling lightly that time, and she ran across the road to his house to take the geography book for him, and she held her own schoolbooks under her arm to prevent the rain wetting them, the books with which she had done her lessons. And out of the corner of her eyes she had glimpsed the jack donkey tied across from the house under the mango tree, flexing the long black thing below its belly, like a hand with fist closed. Then running up the steps, she raised her head, saw the schoolmaster's eyes turn from the jack donkey to her face. Saw his thick moustaches, his forehead, saw his mouth half open showing the red inside of his under lip. Knew. She knew, did not know what it was, something was not right, felt it. And suddenly he was very close to her, the smell of him, his maleness was about her, his eyes were fixed on her. His lips were thick and the inside of the under one was red. And then his breath. His breath was over her, and he. He was all over her suddenly. She had not been strong. If she had been strong? Swept off her legs, in his arms now; and he carrying her inside and ridiculously she held her schoolbooks and didn't cry out, didn't beg to be put down. Why? She didn't cry out. Where was her voice? Maybe she was afraid, or too surprised. But she should have realized that with those eyes, things were not right. Then like in a dream, she was being taken into his room, and she didn't cry out. Even then she didn't. Didn't cry out. Maybe it was a seizure she had. Fear. And didn't know. Didn't cry out, didn't struggle until afterwards in the bigness and hurt of it and then she tossed out of a wave of reborning and fear and pain and need and death. Out of a valley and down a mountain she had gone not knowing where she had been or where she was until she saw him panting, his lips half parted, his nostrils widened and his grin, over her. She knew herself then, turned and spit on him, ran outside, gathering her clothes around her, forgetting the silly books, out into the rain and the gathering dusk.

She knew that she should tell her father. It was the right thing to do. But she couldn't. Her father would kill. She thought about Pedro. She wished that she would die. But she knew that she wouldn't die: just wishing it was not enough. And she didn't want to see Pedro now. Not now. Maybe not ever. She couldn't tell Pedro. She could tell him? No. She couldn't tell Pedro. She would have to bear it. Carry it and bear it. Bear it without even knowing what it was she was asking herself to bear. And about going back to school? She could not leave. She would have to go back to school as usual as if nothing had happened. She did not dare trust herself to think up an excuse. She must go back. No one must know. Not Pedro. Not her father. For their own good, and not for any sin on her part. She must hold it, this pain and rape. She must bear it, and go back to school as if nothing had happened. Something terrible and big had happened. She knew it as she knew the pain between her thighs. She knew it as she knew the sickness and the fear in her heart.

Christiana cried a little harder now, then she wiped her eyes, and walked home without her schoolbooks. She did not know something terrible enough to wish on the schoolmaster.

Chapter Eight

I

Walking under the broiling Sunday-afternoon sun above Kumaca, in the company of Consantine Patron, Francis Assivero, the father of Pedro, was many times tempted to slacken his collar and remove the tie choking at his throat. But although perspiration broke out again and again on his face, and ran down the skin of his back to wet the white shirt underneath his black jacket, and although his brown shoes newly taken on credit at the shop of Dardain were not yet broken in and pinched his toes, he knew that he had to endure every maddening discomfort because of the dignity of the occasion, for his own dignity, and for the sake of his son.

He was carrying in a brown, wooden jewel-box, a treasure of his earlier and prosperous times, a letter which his son had written to Paulaine Dandrade. He held the box in his right hand, and in his left his handkerchief which was damp now with the perspiration he had wiped from his face.

'Your Pedro will be fortunate to have such a girl as wife,' Consantine Patrone said.

Patron wore neither jacket nor tie, but his shirt was buttoned at the wrists and at the neck. Yet about him there was something that made him look dignified and fit for the occasion. Maybe it was the way he walked, or the words that came out of his mouth, or the set of his face with its high brow and hawk's nose. Maybe it was because he was a big man and everybody knew his name, and they knew his face in Valencia even beyond the gayelles, and in many places in Zanilla.

'She is a nice girl,' Francis Assivero, the older of the two men, said. 'But Pedro is a good boy too.'

'I wonder how Paulaine will take it. That girl, since the death of his wife, has been like a mother to him and his sons.'

'You mean that my son is not good enough?'

'I do not say that, Francis. Why do you get so touchy? Everybody in Kumaca knows that at one time you owned half the village, and had many, many gamecocks.'

90

Assivero wiped his face, and shifted the jewel-box to the other hand.

'They know better that I do not have hardly anything now, and that I am too often drunk with rum from the shop of Dardain.'

'You say that?'

'I say it. I know. It is when your head reaches where your knees used to be that you get to understand the ways of people. Then it is very late. But it is life, eh, Mr Consantine.'

'It is life,' Consantine Patron said.

'But I do not doubt Pedro will be fortunate to have such a girl for wife. In Kumaca, everybody give her a good name ... In my days now ... In my days, I would give them the biggest wedding in Kumaca. Ah!'

'It can still be a big wedding,' Consantine Patron said.

'I would go to Port-of-Spain to buy such a suit for my son, and there would be so much to drink ... Whisky and rum and wines of all description. The whole of Kumaca would be drunk ... But what is the use of this talking now. I am not the Francis Assivero who had a name.'

Consantine Patron didn't say anything, and Francis Assivero turned to him.

'It is life, eh, Consantine.'

'It is life,' Patron said.

Francis Assivero wiped the perspiration from his face, and the edges of the handkerchief strayed near his eyes. They went on walking, Consantine Patron with his long leisurely strides, and old Assivero with his short, quick steps, his free arm swinging in brisk arcs.

They were going past the schoolhouse now. Children were playing on a swing which the schoolmaster had persuaded the village council to purchase. Near by, some of the bigger children, girls included, were playing cricket with a bat made from a dried coconut branch, and a ball from the rounded knot made from bamboo's root. A few children and two old men, one smoking a pipe, stood watching the game. Also looking on were the schoolmaster and Dardain, both seated in the gallery of the schoolmaster's house, both with glasses in their hands.

Consantine Patron walked with head held straight, but Francis Assivero felt his eyes dragged in the direction of the men on the gallery. He waved to them and they returned his wave. He walked on a bit uneasily.

'They are very thick together, those two,' Consantine Patron said.

'Maybe they talk the business of the village, eh?'

'Yes,' Consantine Patron said with a laugh that was not really a laugh. 'Yes.'

Francis Assivero laughed too, in innocence, not really grasping what Consantine had laughed at, but laughing because he did.

'I keep my hands clear of the village council and those two,' Consantine said.

'It is not good, the village council?' Assivero asked.

'Those two, I do not trust.'

'Mr Consantine, you are a big man. If they do bad, you should go to the council and see that they do right, eh. I for me is an ignorant man and cannot read even. But Paulaine is there with them in the village council.'

'Paulaine! They do Paulaine what they like. He supports everything this schoolmaster brings. Look at the fête for Easter. I hear it did not turn out good. Imagine, they want to make speech at such a time when everybody looking to have a good time. Did you like how the Easter fête was, Francis?'

'It was not bad.'

'It was not bad, you say. Was it like the fête we accustomed to have here in Kumaca? Or you do not want to answer?'

'It was not the same, Consantine. There were changes, but they say is for the better. It is progress.'

'Who say that?'

'The schoolmaster, and Paulaine.'

'I tell you, he is making Paulaine an ass. Paulaine cannot see that.'

'Paulaine is a good man. He is very fair in his dealings,' Assivero said.

'I do not say Paulaine is bad. Paulaine is blind. He sees what he wants to see. He thinks this schoolmaster is another god. And this reading and writing, the bread of heaven.'

'You say that, and you can read, Mr Consantine?'

'I can read, yes. But writing and reading is not all.'

'You should come to the meetings of the council. It is for everybody.

They ask many times, why does Consantine Patron stay away. Some say you are busy. Some say you feel yourself too great for the village council.'

'Those are fools who say that. Those two already have them in their hands. Even Paulaine is in their hands. And you see now the schoolmaster buys a white horse, and rides it like a governor.'

'He still do many things for the village, eh?'

'Yes, Francis. A lot, he do. Soon he will change this village so you yourself will not know it. Look – I better not talk of this man . . . Tell me, why does he have to buy a white horse? Eh?'

'Maybe he is a busy man, Consantine. Listen! With these intelligent men, you do not know the reason why they do a thing. I remember in the time of the Water Scheme project down at Valencia when I was working, there was a white man in charge. He come from England. And he comes to work, and is always walking about in the rain. He does not carry an umbrella. He does not wear a hat. I ask, what is this? They tell me he is a man of intelligence. It is the way of such people, they say. And there was in Valencia, Pemberton the son of Rodney, who went to study in England, they say. And he read many books, and will walk the road and not say a word, would just look at a leaf. He picked a leaf off a tree and look at it, then put it in his pocket. Not a word. It is the way of such men. But really, this schoolmaster do some good work in Kumaca. We cannot complain. Is it not he that responsible for the road that is to come from Valencia? Some of the men up here will get work to do on the road. My son Pedro too says that as soon as they begin to take on men, he would go down and get a job. Don't you think that the road is a good thing for Kumaca?'

'It is a good thing. I do not say it is not,' Consantine Patron said, losing interest now in the discussion.

Francis Assivero asked, 'Do you know when they begin work?'

'Next month, I hear. They are right now settling the matter of where the road is to pass. Government will pay a good price for the lands that Dardain owns nearly all by himself.'

'If they are to begin soon, I will tell Pedro to keep himself ready. He is just now taking a wife, and must make himself a man.'

It was very quiet at the house of Paulaine Dandrade, and Francis Assivero was relieved now to be out of the sun and walking up the shaded path to the house. Christiana was sitting on the trunk of a fallen samaan tree in the shade near the cocoa house. She had her elbows on her knees, and propped up her chin with the palm of one hand. She was very quiet, and seemed lost in thought.

'Ha ha, you are dreaming, child,' Consantine Patron said with a smile. They had walked up almost to the girl and she had not noticed them come up.

'Good evening, Mr Consantine, good evening, Mr Francis,' she said hurriedly.

'How are you, Christiana? Is your papa at home?'

'He is in the house,' Christiana said, getting to her feet. 'You can go in.'

Francis Assivero smiled. He said, 'Good. We go to see him now.'

'Fine girl,' Consantine Patron said.

'She has good manners,' Assivero said.

The front door was open, but the two men stood on the narrow gallery, and knocked on the door. Paulaine came to the door, and the men exchanged greetings, then he asked them in.

'How are you, Assivero? It is long since I see you over this side. And Consantine, I hear that your cocks did very well in the battles at Valencia.'

'They did all right. At Valencia they ask me, why Paulaine Dandrade is afraid to bring his cocks to our gayelle? He doesn't fight cocks anymore? I stand up and tell them, Paulaine is afraid of the cocks of Consantine Patron, so he keeps his birds in Kumaca where he will win all the battles.'

Paulaine Dandrade smiled. He said with a laugh, 'You do not say it right. You should say, Paulaine has such good cocks that he allows those of Consantine to fight yours. When you beat Consantine, then your cocks are good enough to go with his in the gayelle. Ha ha!'

The three men laughed.

'Sit down,' Paulaine said.

'In truth, I hear you have a very fast one, Paulaine.'

'It is a good one. I am not putting him in the gayelle as yet.'

'I would tell you a story about fighting cocks,' Assivero said. 'But

94

you will not listen. It was a story they tell me long ago, and I did not listen.'

The two men listened to Assivero, because they knew that he had had some good cocks and that they had aided greatly in his fall.

They waited in silence, intently, and with some sadness that neither of them wanted to show.

'I change my mind,' Assivero said. 'I will not say the story to you. The story is not worth repeating to men with blood in their veins.'

'You say so,' Consantine said.

Consantine Patron sat with his legs crossed at the knees, Assivero sat with the soles of his feet resting on the floor. He held the small jewel-box on one knee, and the palm of his hand rested on the other.

'It is good to sit down' he said. 'It is hot outside today.'

'It is good weather for me,' Paulaine said. 'I have some cocoa drying still. And I will have a little bit of harvest next week.'

'I finish my picking,' Consantine said.

'I find,' Paulaine said, 'that the crop was not good this year.'

'It will not be good next year,' Consantine said. 'It is already June, and rains come as if they do not want to come.'

Francis Assivero said, 'Whenever the weather is not nice, the crop is not good. Sometimes the sun too hot, and chirelle fall off the trees. Sometimes the rain is too much, and the chirelle are water soaked, and rot very easy. I get much of this weather on my little place.'

'The schoolmaster tells that in some countries they can tell when rain is going to fall, and can even control the fall of the rain.'

'How do you do this, Mr Paulaine?'

'They have machines, he says, which go up into the sky, and they can bring the rain.'

Consantine Patron was silent.

'That is a great thing,' Assivero said.

'He says too that in a few years the price of cocoa will drop because there are many countries now producing cocoa. In Africa and other parts.'

'That is what *he* says,' Consantine Patron said. 'Your schoolmaster seems to know about everything.'

'True, Consantine. He has been to places. He even been to Panama,' Paulaine said.

'They have much bananas in Panama,' Assivero said. 'And mosquitoes. My cousin Miguel was in Panama for many years; then he come back.'

'We have talked,' Paulaine said. 'Now let me offer you a drink.'

'Thank you,' Consantine Patron said.

'Thank you,' Assivero said.

Paulaine went for the rum, and according to the custom of the village, he put the bottle on the table, with glasses, a jug of water and an aerated drink.

After each man had poured his own, and they had had their drinks, Francis Assivero took the small wooden jewel-box from his knee. He stood up.

'Mr Paulaine, my son sends a letter to you.'

Paulaine took the box, looked at it, placed it on the wagonette.

'Mr Assivero, I receive the letter of your son.'

It was the way the thing was done.

'He has written the letter for himself,' Consantine Patron said.

'I will read the letter of your son. Let us have another drink.'

They had another drink.

'Do you hear that the road is soon to be opened?' Paulaine said.

'I hear it is next month,' Consantine said. 'How are the arrangements working?'

'Things are in the hands of the schoolmaster. Dardain is helping him.'

'Dardain? That is very good,' Consantine said stiffly.

'With the road now, many of the young men will get some work to do,' Assivero said.

'But more than that,' said Paulaine. 'The village will be opened up. With the road, people will come more often to Kumaca, and we will be able to go down to Valencia and Zanilla and sell our produce.'

'You are not afraid about this opening up, then, Paulaine. Truly?'

'I am not afraid. I am happy because it will be better for the village.'

'What does the schoolmaster say to this?' Consantine asked.

'He too thinks it will be great for the village.'

Consantine Patron shook his head briskly, and a sigh came through his nostrils.

'Soon we will have to pay more taxes, and water rates and the goods will be more expensive.'

'It will be like anywhere else,' Paulaine said. 'The world is like that. We cannot sit down and watch the world go by. These things will happen. Changes must come. Listen – you must come to the meetings of the village council, and listen to the things the schoolmaster tells us. He has often said many wise and wonderful things. Why do you not come to the meetings, Consantine?'

'You know how busy I am, Paulaine. And what place is there for me? You are there, and Dardain, and your schoolmaster who says such wise and wonderful things.'

'You do not understand, I think, Consantine.'

'I understand, Paulaine. Why do you let the schoolmaster handle everything?'

'He is capable, and he has his horse which can take him very quickly to Valencia. And there is Dardain with him.'

'*Dardain!*'

'Why do you not come to the meetings, Consantine? You will see how things are done. You will be able also to give us your ideas. Eh? Mr Assivero attends our meetings. How do you find them, Assivero?'

'They are good. Good. Maybe the schoolmaster is at the head of things, and talks, but he says things that are good, and which nobody else can say.'

'Why not come, Consantine?' Paulaine asked.

'I think, Paulaine, that sometimes it is good for someone to remain on the outside and watch how things are going. Such a person will see many things which you cannot see on the inside.'

'What you mean?' Paulaine asked quickly. 'What is there to see?'

'I do not mean anything. I just watch how things going.'

'Ah, Consantine, you are your own man,' Paulaine said. 'Let us have another drink.'

They had the drink. Paulaine turned to Assivero.

'I will read the letter of your son, and you will hear from me.'

They were ready to leave now.

'Good evening, then,' Assivero said. 'I wait to hear from you.'

'Good evening,' Paulaine said. 'And Consantine, you must think about coming to the meetings of the council. It can do a man like you no harm.'

'I will think about it,' Consantine Patron said. 'Good evening. Paulaine.'

The two men left the house and walked down the path in silence.

A ground lizard was washing its face in the loose earth at the side of the track, and a dragonfly hovered over the fence near where the goat was tied. The two men walked leisurely now. Francis Assivero was first to speak.

'Well, that is one part finish,' he said.

'And with no fuss,' Consantine said. 'In time a man will take himself a wife and have no fête, even.'

'You think so?' Assivero asked.

'In America, they say it is already so. The two decide, and they go and see the priest and it is settled.'

'That is not natural,' Assivero said. 'A man is going into another world when he is married. And to go so quietly. No. It is too bad. But they save money that way.'

'I think it is because they have no friends to invite,' Consantine said.

'That too is bad. To this wedding I will invite the whole village.'

'In a place like Kumaca, you can do nothing else. Everybody is one.'

'You think the school will hold all the people? Assivero asked.

'If it cannot, then we build a tent outside. I like the feeling a tent gives at a wedding. It gives a feeling of holiness.'

'The time I married,' Assivero said, 'we had three tents. It was the biggest wedding ever in Kumaca. From Mamoral and Zanilla and Maracas and Valencia, people come.'

'Yes,' Consantine Patron said, 'the people still talk about that wedding.'

Assivero cocked his ear like he was listening for some distant sound.

He said, 'Times goes. A man get old. A man get wise after he make himself a fool. You ask yourself, what is the use for me to get this wisdom and I cannot use it.'

'Why you think?' Consantine asked gently.

'I think it is to make a man happy and to make you sad as you look back and see how your life was, and understand how things go. And you have a son now like Pedro, and what can you tell him. He must learn his own wisdom and make his own happiness ... Always we go over our sadness, and only a little remember our happy moments.'

Consantine Patron listened to Assivero, and to his ears, the older man's voice was like an evening with the murmuring of a tired stream, with the scratching of dry bamboo leaves falling from the overhanging trees, with the sound of water dripping off trees, hitting the earth or a cushion of dried leaves, after the rain had ceased.

Near the schoolhouse, a small boy was peeing against the fence upon which two birds were hunched, watching him. The schoolmaster was now alone on his front gallery. Consantine and Assivero returned his wave, and Consantine thought: Maybe I am wrong about this man. Maybe he is a good fellow, and it is true that I am envious of his popularity. Maybe I should go to the meetings of the village council.

'It is a fine evening,' Assivero said.

'And dusk is coming,' Consantine said.

II

Now Paulaine Dandrade finished smoking the cigarette, and went to the wagonette. He looked at the small, wooden box, then took it into his hands. It was a beautiful trinket box of mahogany with many fine carvings on its surface. It smelled ancient, and grand and a little holy. He lifted the brass hook out of the eye, opened it, and took out the sheet of paper which was tied in a roll, with a ribbon. He untied the ribbon, then took the letter, went to the rocking-chair and sat down. He read the letter once, then he read it again. Then again he read it. He folded it, tied it with the ribbon, replaced it in the box, and as he stood there fixing the brass hook into the eye to close the box, there came a breath of silence about the room, and the smell of lilies and cedar blossoms, and he thought of his wife, and he turned, looked through the window where the greenness was turning to grey as the last sunshine died, and his eyes clouded a little and he blinked rather quickly and turned to go into the kitchen where he would find his daughter Christiana.

Paulaine went quietly from the house to the kitchen. Christiana was at the fireside looking at the bake roasting in the pot. She had her back turned to the door, and did not hear her father come in.

'My daughter.'

'Yes, Papa.'

'You are so quiet.'

'I am alone here, Papa.'

Paulaine smiled a tender, quiet smile, and with the spirit of that smile in his voice, he said: 'I bring news that will make you not so quiet. Where are the boys? They have not come back from playing cricket yet?'

'They have gone for the goats, Papa.'

'Good.'

Paulaine sat on the bench, and he looked for a moment at his daughter now tending the bake. And although she was conscious of his gaze, she kept her eyes on the bake which she held with a cloth, and rolled gradually on its edges along the pot, so that the sides would be well cooked.

'I have received a letter from the son of Francis Assivero. Pedro.'

Christiana turned the bake over. She did not look at her father.

'Yes, Papa.'

'He writes that he loves you. He desires you to be his wife. He has made a very good letter. I did not suspect he could write so well.'

'He learns very quick, Papa.'

'That is true. I have watched him. He is young and very quick. What sort of person is he, you know?'

'He is very funny, Papa – sometimes. And he is serious too. And when I see him busy, and now he is often dreaming. But he makes fine things with his hands, and he plays very well on the flute.'

'I have heard him play.'

Paulaine got off the bench and went nearer to his daughter, and with her, watched the bake.

'My daughter, you have reached age now. And if it is your desire, then I will give my permission and my blessings. A young person has his life before him. Francis Assivero, the boy's father, was once a very

100

big man in Kumaca, but his son now will have to work hard to make something of himself. It is good when one works hard with his eyes on something before him. If you can make a living with Pedro, if you can make the times when he comes home pleasant, and make him feel like a man then it will be very good. If a woman feels that she can do these things, then only is it wise to marry a man. Do you feel this way?'

'I know I can make Pedro happy, Papa. But . . .'

'But . . . my child?'

'But I do not want to leave this house now, Papa.'

'Ha, Christiana, we cannot tie you here for ever. It is your life you have. You must go sometime. You have grown very well, and your conduct makes your father proud of you, and all the people in Kumaca have a good name for you. And you have been very good to the boys and to me, and have tended us since your mother died. But, girl, I have heard young Assivero playing the music of his heart on his flute, and I have seen the look on your face when you listen.'

'I do not care to leave this house, Papa.'

'It makes my heart swell, and my head big to hear your words, Christiana. But the boy loves you. He has made a very fine letter with his own pen. Tell me truly, how do you feel?'

'He is in my thoughts, Papa, like the ears in my head. He said to me that he would write. But, Papa . . .'

'You are afraid of what, Christiana? A girl grows. She must become a woman one day. Of the change you are afraid, or of Pedro?'

'I am not afraid of Pedro, Papa.'

'Of the change, then?'

'Not of that.'

'Then what makes you afraid?'

'Who will cook and do the things in the house?'

Christiana took the bake from the pot, and Paulaine went slowly and sat down on the bench.

'Come here, Christiana. And sit down.'

She went and joined her father on the bench.

Paulaine looked carefully into her eyes.

'It is not fair for you to think of these things. You have no special responsibility here now. It is my responsibility.'

'Papa.'

'What is it?'

Paulaine looked at his daughter, and saw the set of her face, and the quivering of her nostrils, and the flood breaking in her eyes.

'Why do you cry for, child?'

Christiana's lips trembled and stretched across her face, and she sucked the air into her nostrils, with quick sniffing sounds. She couldn't tell her father why she was crying. She would have liked to tell him so that he would know of the schoolmaster now, and the schoolbooks left on the floor near the bed that evening with the rain and the suddenness, and the jack donkey across the road, and the night of pain and two burnings. Couldn't tell him. He would take up his gun and walk to the house of the schoolmaster. Then police! The police had come to Kumaca once and had taken Carrera the son of old Leo who lives near the river, in a house now grown silent and old like rotted immortelle wood, and the old man silent too and very old and bent since the police came and took the son who, they say, went into the town of Zanilla, and there in a fight with a man who with some companions had beaten him sometime before, with a cutlass chopped from the elbows both the man's hands. The police must not come for her father. What would happen to the boys? What would happen to little Humphy? She could not tell him. Could not. Must not.

'You do love the boy?' Paulaine asked.

'I love him, Papa.'

'Then ... then it is all right. Your mother cried too when we had our time. And Christiana, I think he would make you a fitting husband. And you must be a wife to him to lift him up and to lighten the times of his life and have his children and bring them up and teach them how it is to live.'

'Yes, Papa.'

'And do not think of this house. You have my permission to marry, and I will do what is to be done in the house here. Do not cry. You say he is intelligent, and he makes music and tells jokes. All these things are necessary for you to have happiness in a home. You can make some fine moments in his life for him. And we, your brothers and I, love you, Christiana. You will marry the boy?'

102

'I will marry him, Papa.'

To herself she said: I will tell him. I will tell Pedro so that he will know. No! Oh, God, no! Cannot tell him. Must not tell him! Yes, I will tell him. He must know.

But no. She could not tell him. She must keep it, bear it, live with it. What other way was there?

Paulaine Dandrade said, 'Then I will write to him and give my reply.'

And in his heart now there was a feeling of softness and of pride at the tears of his daughter. For it is the good girl that cries at such a time.

Part Three

Chapter Nine

I

It was the time of the *petit carême* now, and in this pause, this summer's breath in the midst of wet weather, the forest bees came quick in blue sunshine to new blossoms, and fresh-feathered birds flew, flitted with song and love-calls from boughs to the wild flowers. In cocoa fields, the guardian immortelles were in sporadic bloom, and farmers were busy picking the little harvest of cocoa which they hoped to dry before the rains commenced again.

Kumaca was beautiful at this time of year, with yellow unclung leaves drifting in the wind, pouis spotting the hillsides with fistfuls of gold, and parrots squawking like matriarchal fishwives, crossing low over the forest where somersaulting monkeys howled in dark voices. In the village, all the talk was of the road which was to come through from Valencia. Matters had been settled by the schoolmaster, and the surveyors had begun work, but it would be two, maybe three weeks before the eight or ten men chosen from Kumaca would begin work. It was a fine time of year in Kumaca, with old men in the evenings, sitting under shade trees, smoking their pipes and remembering to each other friends dead and gone, and debating who would outlive whom, and what sort of cocoa crop there would be next year. And there was the crowing of the fighting-cocks in backyards, being prepared for the cockfights, and the planning of the wedding between Pedro and Christiana.

Now in the office of the schoolmaster, which was used as a confessional whenever the priest was at Kumaca, the daughter of Paulaine Dandrade knelt on one side of the two blackboards which served as a screen to separate the confessor from the priest. She was trembling, and her lips were pressed tightly together. Through the space between the two blackboards, she could see the large, pink ear of the priest, like the inside of a halved, magnified cashew seed, stuck to the side of his head. His face was averted from her, but the ear gazed, and it was through it that the voice of the priest seemed to come like a night wind now through leafless trees.

'What is it you say, child?'

These days, the voices of the village women filled her ears. They had looked at her when she went down by the river to wash and had commented: 'Girl, you fulling up already. Child, you spreading . . . This Pedro is not making joke at all, eh . . .' And she, unvirgin, had smiled in innocence until the heaviness stiffened in her breasts, and the awkwardness lumped in her stomach. She should have told her father. Or Pedro. She should have told Pedro.

She answered the priest now.

'I am with child, Father.'

The priest bowed his head. She watched his ear go down like an empty fishing boat between the waves. His hands came away from his knees, his fingers touched his brow, rested there. His voice came soft now, like the tread of a tired cat over dried bamboo leaves.

'Why could you not wait, child?'

'It was not by my will, Father.'

The forehead of the priest rubbed against the fingers of his left hand.

'Always . . . It is always not of your will. The boys play with the girls . . . then it happens . . . Not of your will.'

He sat there in a sort of twilight and sadness.

'It was not the boys, Father,' she said.

'It was a man, then?'

And now she thought that the priest's ear was a pink bowl with an eye in its centre.

'Yes, Father.'

'Does that improve the situation? Tell me, is he married?'

'I do not think so, Father.'

'You do not *think* so, Father! Do you not know *that* much?'

'I do not know, Father.'

The priest, tiredly, then suddenly giving way to his rage and desire to hurt:

'How would you know? But it is a man. Do you know him?'

'I know the man, Father.'

The priest's head bowed, two fingers drummed on his brow.

108

The girl said: 'It is the schoolmaster, Father.'

The fingers stopped drumming on the brow. The head paused, then it came up and the hands dropped away. With an effort, the priest kept his eyes averted.

'Do you know what you are saying, girl?'

'It is true, Father.'

'Girl, are you certain?'

'In his house. After lessons. I was running in from the rain . . . And a donkey was across the road. And the schoolmaster . . . the schoolmaster . . .'

The back of the priest straightened, and the priest groaned audibly. His voice was tired and very soft.

'Pray with me. Pray, child. Hail, Mary, Full of Grace . . .'

'Hail, Mary, Full of Grace . . .'

'The Lord is with thee . . . Blessed art though among women . . .'

'The Lord is with thee . . .'

And saying the words now, Christiana remembered her school-books, and how she had found them the day after, piled neatly on the table at which she sat at the school. And she could hear now the sound of Pedro's flute, with the rain and bird-calls in it, and she saw her father's face when she was crying there that evening in the kitchen. And her mother. She saw her mother now sitting on top of a big rock in the deep water of the river in the forest. She saw her mother as she remembered her, with her sad, quiet face and long eyelashes.

'And at the hour of our death,' she repeated mechanically.

'Amen.'

'Amen.'

And now the priest's ear gazed at her, and she saw now that it was a pool, a deep pool and her mother was sitting on the bank there, waiting for her, in her long white dress . . . waiting for her.

She heard the priest's voice coming out of the river of his ear.

'And you were not willing?'

'I was afraid, Father. He was so strong, and I was surprised. I struggled too late. I should have told my father. But I was afraid.'

'Why were you afraid?'

'My father is too good. He would get himself in trouble without end. He has a gun, Father. He would shoot the schoolmaster. And I did not tell Pedro either, although he has written to marry me, and it is arranged.'

'Why?'

'For the same reason, Father. And I did not know what to do. And there was no one to tell.'

The girl knelt twisting her handkerchief around her finger.

'This boy, do you love him?'

'I love him, Father.'

'And he has not . . .? You and he . . . have not . . .?'

'No. No, Father. No.'

'Nor any other boy . . . or . . . man?'

'No, Father.'

'Oh, Holy Virgin, pray for us,' the priest sighed. 'And you have not told this boy?'

'It is to you alone I tell this now, Father.'

'Why have you kept this big . . . this terrible secret? Why, child?'

'My father would kill if he knows what was done to me. And Pedro also would do something terrible. And I was afraid. I do not want them to get in trouble.'

'You go still for lessons?'

'I go to school. If I do not go, I would have to tell my father why. Then he would find out, and it would be terrible, Father.'

'Only once it happened?'

'He asked me if I were not coming over for lessons after that. But I did not go.'

'But there was this once?'

'Yes, Father.'

'And you were not willing?'

'I was not willing.'

'It is a dangerous secret you have kept child,' the priest said, his tongue rolling over the R's in the words dangerous and secret. 'How old are you?'

'I am seventeen this month, Father.'

'Pray to Our Holy Mother. I will pray for you.'

'Yes, Father.'

'You say you love this boy?'

'Yes, Father.'

'And you are afraid that your father also would get in trouble?'

'Yes, Father.'

'I will pray for you, child.'

'What must I do, Father?'

'Child,' the priest began wearily. 'Child, I will pray.'

And in the priest's ear she saw the deep dark pool, and she was there in the pool, with her mother, and her mother was in her white dress, and was putting her arms about her, and was going to kiss her.

'You love this boy?'

'Yes, Father.'

'Very much? Enough to give him up?'

'I love him, Father.'

'Perhaps you will have to give him up. It might be the only way. But I will pray.'

'Should I tell my father now, Father?'

The priest bowed his head.

'In my hands. It is in my hands.'

'Yes, Father.'

'And – pray.'

When Christiana had gone, Father Vincent leaned back in the chair, and looked up above him, then he bent his head into his hands. His face was very red, and very hot, and he didn't know what prayer to say. And it came to him that he needed a miracle. A miracle was very hard to make, very hard to come by, and he thought that perhaps the days of miracles were gone, but he didn't want to think this, because he was a priest, and priests had faith, priests believed. Yet he thought it, and felt sad, and useless, and less than a priest. But he was a priest, had to be ... But now another woman was coming to make her confession.

II

All during the other confessions, this thing rested on the priest and weighed him down; his sadness was not only for the girl, and her father, and the boy whom she was pledged to marry: it was a sadness for himself, and for all mankind. His faith was not great enough, and to pray seemed inadequate – not action enough, and as priest he was not good enough. But God knew how he tried. God knew the thoughts with which he struggled, and the doubts he tried to stifle. God knew. And now the priest smelled blood, saw how it flowed, saw how violence raised its voice and shouted from the very groin of man. Saw wars and slaughter and the grotesque face of anger. Father Vincent saw his dreams of a better life in this world rise up like the sacrificial incense and disappear, leaving only its smell in the region of the altar and on his ritual garments. And now the vision of his own priesthood and usefulness was to him like ashes in his teeth. But what could he do, only as priest? It was only God riding on his thunder, with his voice big with the sound of many waters to put an end to it all. He could not help but wonder whether God did not look on, did not see all, but he left man to work out his salvation for himself.

During the mass that day, the voice of the priest was like the tired trickle of a drying stream. He said the words slowly, and did the various actions connected with the mass with the fumbly movements of a vacant-minded old man in the trance of his decline. When it was over, he was relieved, but he had to see the schoolmaster, and this did not lessen his sadness and his guilt feelings.

And now it was time almost to leave Kumaca. He had finished shaking the rough hands of the villagers, and mumbling in his trance of sadness the mechanical words of goodbye. Outside, the acolytes were waiting near the donkeys in the rough pasture across from the school, and Benn, who was not very drunk today, was propped up at the base of the mango tree, with his hat pulled low over his eyes, smoke swirling from his cigarette, about his head.

Now the schoolmaster faced the priest, with his bright smile and his many teeth, his right hand extended for the priest to take.

Standing there, Father Vincent looked at this man, somehow expecting to see on his face, to discern in his attitude, some hint, some sign of change, some glimpse of the degeneration into which he had so obviously sunk. No change that the eye could see. No change. The same jowly grin, bead-like eyes behind the spectacles, the proper suit, the proper tie, the cultured bowing from the waist. No change. The face that you have learned, and that smile taught you, thought the priest, clasping his own hands behind his back, ignoring the schoolmaster's proffered hand, and making ready to speak, while the schoolmaster in subtle concession and pretended ignorance, withdrew his hand, and still with the same face, giving nothing away, he spoke before the priest could get his words out.

He had a not unpleasant speaking voice, and took his time with his words, conscious of his power over them.

'You have good weather for the journey back, Father.'

'Yes, we have good weather, Mr Warrick.'

'I'd say, Father, that the weather has been rather good of late. Makes one think of picnics on hillsides – of course, not on these thickly forested hills of ours.'

'Mr Warrick.'

'Yes, Father.'

'Do you like Kumaca?'

'It is a little quiet, Father. But one can do some work here. I like the place. I am happy to say that work has begun on the road from Valencia. The surveyors have started, and next week some of the men from Kumaca will join the work gang.'

'I can see that you are very pleased about that,' Father Vincent said.

The priest was thinking: No, there is nothing in your face. Nothing in your voice to show. Yes, you have been well taught, and have been a too good student.

'So you like Kumaca, Mr Warrick . . .? Do you get along well with the people?'

'Father, it will be no exaggeration to say that they love me.'

The priest bowed his head.

'I see . . . Yes, yes, yes. And you would not like to leave?'

'Not now, Father. No.'

'And the children at the school. How are they getting on?'

'Improving rapidly, Father. There are a few who even now find it difficult to remember the A B C, but by and large, I would say that improvement is evident in every sphere. In speech, in deportment, in discipline. Father, the young men now sit before the shop and read and discuss the writings in the newspapers which I bring them, and the standard of debate at meetings of the village council is unbelievably high.' The schoolmaster's voice was filled with a sense of wonder.

The priest's voice was very dry.

113

'In the school. The teacher, your assistant. The young lady ...? Help me with her name ... Miss ...?'

'Miss Dandrade.'

'Yes. Miss Dandrade.'

'She is coming along, Father. Slowly. Rather slowly.'

'Surprising. On the last occasion, you said that she was doing excellent work.'

'I did, Father. But at that time the children she taught knew much less. Now she is finding it a bit difficult to keep pace with them. The children have improved tremendously, Father.'

'I seem to have gathered that you gave her private lessons at your home – Miss Dandrade, that is ...'

'I have been helping her with lessons, yes, Father.'

'And she has not been responding ... Well! Then maybe we had better replace her, eh, Mr Warrick?'

'If we can find a proper replacement, yes, Father.'

The priest flexed his fingers behind his back and sighed through clenched teeth. He thought: He agrees so easily to this, eh. And shows nothing. Ah.

And because of the schoolmaster's complete self-control, the priest felt a greater sense of frustration and guilt. The man was too clever. He was too much. He was too well schooled.

Now the priest looked very carefully at the schoolmaster.

'I did speak to her, you know, Mr Warrick. She seems to be in a bit of trouble. Perhaps this has been responsible for her attitude to her work.'

'What, Father?'

'The trouble. Did she not tell you of it?'

'No, Father.'

'She did not? I think she should have. It is something you should know. She is with child. I think she should have told you, Mr Warrick.'

Father Vincent watched his schoolmaster squinting horrified surprise behind his spectacles, listened for him to speak. But he said no word.

'What is your relationship like with her?' the priest asked.

'My relationship with her, Father? Is like that of a teacher to a

114

student. But she is very quiet, and like so many of these country children, keeps to herself.'

'And you yourself have not noticed that she is with child?'

With a grin, the schoolmaster: 'I do not notice these things very well, Father.'

'Are you surprised? I always thought that she was a fairly steady girl. I mean, not the careless village girl type.'

'I am rather surprised, Father. I am, indeed.'

And now the priest sprang.

'And what do you propose to do now?'

'Beg your pardon, Father.'

Tired, carefully, the priest: 'What should be done now?'

'She will have to cease teaching, Father. For the good of the children.'

'Of course, Mr Warrick. But what are *you* going to do?'

'I, Father?'

'Yes, Mr Warrick, you. You have sown the seed, haven't you? Haven't you, Mr Warrick?'

Now to his mounting anger, the priest bent only a little then he turned away, brought up one hand and ran fingers through his hair.

The schoolmaster's face had changed so imperceptibly, and had reverted with such subtle ease, that there seemed to have been no change in expression at all.

'Mr Warrick!' the priest cried in a fierce whisper, only to see the schoolmaster with a look of pained, stupid inquiry, considering (so the priest thought) whether he (the priest) were sane.

And now with anger hovering in the background of his words, Father Vincent said:

'Mr Warrick. The trust of the villagers? The integrity of the Church? Your own integrity? The work you have been doing here? The innocence of the child? All these have you ignored? Mr Warrick?'

The countenance of the schoolmaster changed to penitent hopefulness. The priest kept his hands clasped behind his back. Physical violence was not entirely out of his ambit. The anger fought him, but he overpowered it, and was very gentle now as if afraid to tempt himself, tempt his anger.

'You have been weak, Mr Warrick,' the priest said, as to a child

115

who cannot understand the extent of his wrongdoing, and the terrible repercussions of his actions.

And without crumbling, in a sort of defiant penitence, the schoolmaster answered in his cultured tone:

'I have been weak, Father.'

'Do not boast of your weakness,' the priest said crisply. He spoke slowly now, as if to regulate his breathing. 'This is bad for the village. For the Church. For all that you appeared to work for. It is better that you leave.'

After the silence, the schoolmaster raised his head that had been bowed.

'I have done much work here, Father. I have much work to complete.'

Father Vincent again put up a fight with his anger, and though he was victorious, when he spoke this time he wasn't so gentle.

'So you would not like to leave, then?'

'I would not.'

There was wonder in the priest's voice, and a sense of butting his head against a stone wall, and a feeling that somewhere along the way he had missed out on some very important factor.

'You will face this thing? You will make it right with the villagers?'

He broke from the irony of his tone to a despairing cry: 'This thing cannot be made right . . . Only a miracle . . .'

'I can marry the girl, Father.'

And because the priest had uttered the word miracle, and because in his head now were thoughts of his own faith, or lack of it, and because he wanted to believe – not the words of the schoolmaster, but believe again, believe in miracles, in acts of faith, against his judgment he spoke now with some hope, and with a sense of miracle in his brain.

'Do you not know that she is promised to another?'

'It is only by marrying her,' the schoolmaster said, 'that I can remove some of the hurt from her, and some of the shame from myself.'

And refusing – no, fearing – to trust himself, and still with a sense of miracle in his brain, the priest whispered: 'Can that be done?'

116

'Father, I have done wrong. But you are a priest. A man is weak. The flesh overpowers the spirit.'

And the priest edging himself to a compromise:

'And you could not resist the temptation? Was it because you were alone?'

'I have not been strong, Father. I have been lonely also, but it was my weakness.'

The priest edging closer:

'And the girl. Do you think she will marry you?'

'I would be willing to marry her, Father.'

And the priest testing the possibilities of his compromise:

'You have undermined the dignity of your profession. You have taken advantage of your position in this village.'

'It has never happened to me before, Father.'

'The girl was unwilling, wasn't she?'

'I did not think so then, Father.'

'But you know that now?'

'I will marry her, Father.'

'But that does not appear possible.'

'Father, do you not say that all things are possible, with God? . . . There is no other way I can right this wrong. If I leave now I would be just as bad. I have truly been a great help to the village.'

And now this challenge, these words: All things are possible with God, this idea of miracle rooted itself in the brain of the priest. He knew that he should be stronger, should be as just as the avenging angel with flaming sword and hell. But because of his faith or non-faith, and the idea of miracle, he was weak or maybe it was strong, and a priest. So he indulged himself.

'You cannot right any wrong,' the priest said, again testing himself, testing the man before him, and playing to his miracle and his faith.

'Not even if I repent, Father? And pray, and ask forgiveness, and marry the girl?'

'Mr Warrick,' the priest said, hiding his anxiety. 'Mr Warrick, you trifle with me.'

'No, Father.'

'I beg of you, do not trifle with me, Mr Warrick.'

'I am at your mercy, Father. I am sorry. I would like to do the best I can. But what can I do?'

'I will pray for you, Mr Warrick.'

'I will like to marry the girl, Father.'

'Will she accept you? And will this be acceptable to all concerned? Those are the questions,' the priest said.

'I can try to satisfy with my good intentions, Father. It is the best that I can do.'

And now, because of the insecure faith of a priest, and the hope of a miracle, Father Vincent gambled his experience against a possibility, against a miracle. Because of his own insecure faith.

'Mr Warrick,' the priest said, not daring to believe that he was actually giving way to a possibility. 'Mr Warrick . . .'

'Yes, Father.'

'For your sake, for Kumaca's sake, for the girl's sake, and the boy's and the sake of Paulaine Dandrade who fought me to have you brought here, I give you this opportunity to attempt to right this terrible wrong that you have done. I will be coming back to Kumaca very soon. Maybe next week.'

'Yes, Father. Thank you, Father.'

The priest looked outside and saw that Benn had left the base of the mango tree and was now standing near to the saddled donkeys.

'I go now, Mr Warrick, and I beg of you, pray.'

'Yes, Father.'

On the way back to Valencia, the priest was silent and very thoughtful. He seemed to be enveloped in an aloneness beyond that given him by his gown and priesthood. His mood dominated the small group, and pushed each individual back upon himself. Even the acolytes were quiet. They journeyed along the track, with the sound of monkeys howling in the high forest.

'Your face is very sad, priest,' Benn said.

'Time . . . My age is catching up with me,' Father Vincent said, trying to smile.

'It was in the prayers you said at the school too.'

'Then you were present at the mass?'

'I find myself at the school, and I listen to your words.'

'How did they affect you?' the priest asked, hopefully.

Benn said, 'I feel more that it is useless, I and these donkeys and these hills.'

After a while, Father Vincent said: 'It is faith that you lack.'

'Faith, priest?'

'It is faith that the whole world lacks,' Father Vincent said.

'I had a handsome black horse, Father. In good faith I give it to a man who tells me he wants to buy it. I say, I give it to you. And that man who never had a mother – that man took my horse and shoot my pretty black horse. I cannot believe it. Priest, I say now that a man when he has the power is a beast, and a dog when he doesn't. Priest, I say that the world is a sad place . . .'

Benn chuckled now as if enjoying a very private joke. He said:

'Suddenly, I think that it is not so bad with me and these donkeys. And it is good that I can get drunk; though I cannot understand why a man cannot take a drink, in peace, in the shops of Valencia . . . but perhaps that is good too, eh, priest? Perhaps everything is good, and has its reason.'

Father Vincent's face softened into a tired smile, as he looked at Benn, and thought again about the schoolmaster and the miracle upon which he, priest, waited.

Chapter Ten

I

Although Pedro had written the letter and had received a favourable reply from Christiana's father, he found still that there was a shyness in him whenever he went to the home of Paulaine Dandrade to see his wife-to-be. But this evening it was different. Now with the shafts of sunlight steady on quiet trees, the threat of rain vanishing with the drifting clouds in the sky, there was in him a subtle, new feeling; and thinking about it, Pedro thought: It is because I am to be married, and am a man now. And the very consideration of this discovery, made him feel, in one sense, wise and old, and having been places and seen many things, and in another, very young, too young.

He was going to say goodbye to Christiana now. He was one of the eight men from Kumaca who would be leaving on the following morning for Valencia, to start working on the road. Perhaps he might have preferred not to leave, but with the knowledge now that he was in fact going, leaving, he felt a certain tallness of stature, a certain bigness of heart, a certain sense of purpose and sacrifice. And he could see the two Pedros, his two selves: The one who loved mischief and to play on a bamboo flute, and the other who was going now, poniard in hand, to work at the direction of the surveyors. Yes, he was a man. And thinking this, he thought of his smaller brother, Robert, and wondered when he would get well and walk again. He wished that there was something he could do for Robert.

He went up the path that led to the house of Mr Paulaine. Two young kids butted at the breasts of the ewe, then rushed furiously to suckle. The ground doves flew up. In the yard, Christiana was taking clothes off a line. Pedro stood and looked at her go about her task with a quiet, almost careful dreaminess, as if she were doing it all half asleep. Then he continued up to her. He had his flute in his pocket, but now, he did not feel to play it. She turned, saw him, and a quiet, sad, slow smile stretched her face. She stood and waited for him, the bundle of clothes held in her arms.

'Good evening, Christiana.'

'Good evening, Pedro.'

They looked into each other's eyes.

'You are working hard,' he said. 'Where is Mr Paulaine for me to say good evening?'

'They have all gone to the garden, even Humphy. Papa is pruning some trees. Do you want to come inside?'

'I can remain out here if you like.'

'Then I will put down the clothes inside.'

She turned to walk to the house. He followed her to the steps.

'I go to Valencia early in the morning,' he said.

She continued into the house. She did not seem to hear him, and he remained by the steps until she returned.

'I leave tomorrow,' he said again.

She came near to him, and she looked at him, and he went to her and kissed her on the mouth. They kissed and did not speak. They sat on the steps.

'To work with surveyors?' she asked.

'Yes. With the money I get, it will not be difficult to build a house and to buy chairs and tables and things that must go into a house.'

She didn't say anything, looked across the yard to the hills. He followed her gaze. A pair of wild pigeons were mounting high up, wings going very fast.

He said, 'There go the two of us. We are going into a new life.'

They gazed at the birds for a long while, didn't speak. She held his hands. She played with his fingers. He looked at her face.

He said, 'I so love you! It is like my heart wants to be one with yours. I feel it melting inside me, and like sunshine flowing out through cracks and streaming into your heart.'

'No. It is my heart that flows into yours,' she said.

'It is our two hearts flowing into each other, like the light from two suns into a room.'

'Two rooms and two suns,' she said.

She kissed his hand. She had never done that before. He touched her hair.

He said, 'When I go down to that place, I know you will be inside of me, but I will miss you.'

'Will I really be inside of you?'

He traced a finger down the side of her face.

'Where else can you be?'

She pressed his hand to her lips.

'And will I always be there?'

'Always,' he said. 'Always.'

They sat and didn't say anything.

'It is a long time, always,' she said.

'It is for ever you will be inside my heart,' Pedro said.

They were both very quiet, and he felt very soft, like a child or a woman.

'Pedro, play me a tune on your flute,' she asked.

He took the flute from his pocket, and smiled at her.

'It is a little tune I play when my heart is bursting inside me, and I am alone in the evening, thinking of you, and wondering if your heart is bursting and you are thinking of me.'

'Play it for me.'

She looked at his face now as he played the tune. When he was finished playing, they sat and didn't say anything, and he held the flute in his hands, like he didn't know what to do with it.

'When we are together in our house, I will play many tunes for you,' he said after a while.

Her face was soft now like the hillside with the moonlight upon it, then her nostrils quivered, her eyes filled, and teardrops coursed down her cheeks.

'Christiana?'

'Pedro . . .' (Like she wanted to say something.)

'What is it?'

'Pedro . . .' (Still like she wanted to say something.)

'Yes . . .' (Like he expected her to make some revelation.)

'Pedro . . . You are very good, Pedro,' she said.

She cried a little while and he looked on helplessly, then she dried her eyes rubbing her face against the front of his shirt.

'How . . . How long will you be staying?'

'We have to do work. There will be a camp. Maybe we stay for a fortnight. Maybe a month at a time. But I will always come away to see you.'

'You will come to see me?' (Like she had to say something.)

Pedro asked, 'What is it, Christiana?'

'Pedro . . .'

'Yes, Christiana.'

'Pedro.'

'I will come anytime I have a moment,' he said. 'I will make the moments.'

'It is far.'

'It is ten miles. I would run the distance. If I had a horse like the schoolmaster, I could ride. But I do not have a horse.'

'I wish you did not have to go. But you must go. Yes, you must go.

Then she was crying again, struggling with something. He let her cry. He did not ask again what it was she wanted to say.

'As often as I can, I will come to see you,' he said after a while.

'I wish I could come with you, Pedro. I wish I could go away from here with you.'

'It will not be for very long. Then we will be together for ever.'

'Pedro.'

'Christiana.'

'I love you, Pedro.'

'Do not cry,' he said, feeling in that moment very soft and not at all the man he thought he was. 'Do not cry. It will not be for too long.'

'Pedro . . .' (As if she must say it, whatever it was.)

'Come,' he said. 'Let us walk.'

He held her hand and she stood. They walked around by the cocoa house. She looked very sad, and he kissed her. She did not cry. She looked very sad.

'You all right, Christiana?'

She nodded and held his hand tightly. He could sense her fighting to hold back tears. They walked down the path and they kissed and he said goodbye to her. When he left her, he looked back and saw her standing looking at him as if she would call him back. He waved to her, she waved back. She did not call him back.

Christiana stood alone with the dusk gathering and put her hand on her belly. She felt the hardness, and the pain in her went like the teeth of a hand-saw through her entire body, and she bent herself in two, and cried and cried. And in the pool of her tears she saw a bigger pool, a deeper pool, a pool near which her mother stood very quietly waiting on her. She straightened herself very slowly. She would find the pool in the forest. She would find the pool and would go to her mother. She walked slowly back to the yard. She was so sorry that she couldn't bring herself to tell Pedro. She tried to tell him. She was so sorry that she didn't, couldn't. 'Oh, Pedro!' she cried. 'Oh, Pedro!'

II

All week the schoolmaster could not rid himself of it; and could not face it. Though he had ridden his horse hard and long, had flogged the children too much at school, and had drunk too much, too often at Dardain's place and at his own. He could not rid himself of it. He felt pursued, spied on, hated, and despised. He thought again and again of the promise that he had made to the priest. How easy it is to utter words at times. How simple it is to make a promise with your lips.

On the track to Valencia, on the high ground near the landslide and the precipice, he was now sitting on his white horse, watching between the trees the day's last sunshine in the red sky away over Maracas. He was feeling friendless and alone, and was sure that the people of Kumaca did not like him. They did not care about him. You taught their clumsy children to read and write, and to deport themselves properly; you tried to get something into the heads of these flatfaced villagers; and it didn't mean a thing to anybody. Instead, they hated you. That was the thanks you got. Yes, they hated him. To hell with their good evenings and their grins.

He gazed down the precipice to the valley where bamboos were hushing now in the evening's gentle wind, and he could hear the birds turning and twisting, fussing about in the fading light, as tense, overtired children settling down to sleep after a hard day's play ... That was the thanks you got. And although they said to your face that you were pretty good, you weren't pretty good behind your back. Hypocrites. All they wanted was to take from you, not give. He had given much, perhaps too much. And what had he had in return?

Didn't he deserve anything? Dardain was right. He was a bloody scoundrel too, but he was right. A man has a right to himself to take what he wants. Take what you want and to hell with everything else. To hell with the people. To hell with their problems. To hell with their feelings. That was the way. You only got to know people when you fell foul of them. Forgive? Forgive for what? People did not forgive. They traded, and always to their own advantage. That was the essence of their forgiveness – trade. But he did not want their forgiveness. He was bigger than all of them. Bigger! Yes, you are bigger, and will make your demands. They pushed you so that you had to be ruthless. You will not leave Kumaca. The girl will accept you. She is dying for you. She will fall at your feet this very moment if you were to ask her. You are almost a governor in this village. You are like a ruler. You *are* a ruler.

The huge wings of darkness hovered over the land now.

You could take your horse now and push on to Valencia. Get out. Get away. But they need you. At Kumaca they need you. And although he was not sure that he believed anything that he was thinking, he turned the horse's head around to Kumaca, and with the reins held loosely, allowed the animal to pick its own pace. When he reached home, he put the horse into its stall, went inside and uncorked another bottle and poured himself a drink. He had two drinks. He had three drinks, then he began to think what a wonderful fellow he was, and how beloved he was of the people of Kumaca, and how simple and tender-hearted these people were, and what a fine thing it would be to settle in the village and teach their children, guide the destiny of the village, and marry the girl. With these thoughts in mind now, and not really liking to drink alone, he decided at that very hour to go over to his friend Dardain's, and there continue the drinking.

So now the schoolmaster was in the back of the shop which was Dardain's home. They had already had a few drinks between them, and they both felt quite good, and for the first time in – was it five years or seven? – Dardain brought out his old gramophone, played one record, then another. They sat drinking, talking, and remembering while the old records screeched and scratched in the night. And as they talked, Dardain felt himself drawing closer to the schoolmaster, understanding the man better. He felt that he was the man's friend, and opened up his memories to him, told him about his marriage when he was just nineteen to the tall, muscular woman with a hint of moustaches on her lip, and of not having children, and the beatings she gave him – when she beat him, she would sit astraddle him, and shout murder! – and showed him the cut above his left eye where she had butted him that time when he had run away from her and she had trailed him, caught him in the little room, had wrecked the room and taken him back to the house and there had butted him from pillar to post. That was in Arima. And he was always wanting to kill her. He had a hatchet, and one night he planned to kill her while she was sleeping but she always had him on the inside of the bed, so it was not easy to get up and go for the hatchet without disturbing her, for she slept like a cat. Then one day he went to work and didn't go back, went straight to Kumaca, walked to Kumaca where he had remained for ten years before venturing out, had heard that she went insane, died in the mental asylum.

Sharing old memories, telling each other secrets, they were that night the best of friends. So the schoolmaster, perhaps deliberately, saw his opening – or was it all in keeping with the spirit of revelation?

'I am a lonely man, Dardain.'

'You must get a woman, *bouge*.'

'Yes. I drink my loneliness, and it remains in me. If I am to stay here, I need a wife.'

'I am different. I need a woman. But with you, I agree. There are women in the village, not maybe to your taste. They marry early and the others go away. There are some nice girls in Zanilla. But maybe they do not want to leave the town to come to live in this bush. But a man like you should be able to make your persuasion.'

'There is someone here, Dardain.'

'You say there is someone? Here, in Kumaca, I know all the women.'

'There is a girl. But maybe in this village you do not care to let your women marry men who are strangers.'

'You are no more a stranger, schoolmaster. It will be an honour to the village, if you should choose a Kumaca girl. But where is the girl?'

126

'The girl I would choose will be a fine girl anywhere, Dardain.'

'Ah! You do not mean the daughter of Paulaine? Eh . . .? Then you are too late. The son of Francis Assivero write already for her.'

'And what was the reply?'

'It is favourable. They make preparation for the wedding already.'

'That is the one I would choose, Dardain.'

'You will have to think of another one, schoolmaster. There is Isabelle, the second cousin of Consantine Patron. She has no husband again, and a very fine face. And there is Miss Luciana who is nice too. She has the very juicy breasts. Eh?'

'The daughter of Paulaine is the one I would choose.'

'Here is a drink. You do not want to marry in truth. You only call the name of the girl because you know she is already promised.'

The schoolmaster poured himself a drink.

'I am not joking. I would marry her.'

'If the boy had not written the letter . . . then . . . But . . .'

Dardain spread out his hands to show how hopeless the situation was.

'I see now,' the schoolmaster said. 'I have no friends in this village.'

'You know I am your friend, so you pull my leg,' Dardain said. 'You are not serious.'

'Look at my face. Do I look like a man who is joking? Eh?'

'Then, schoolmaster, you are serious about the wrong girl. Miss Luciana has the juicy breasts. She can do everything. If I was not so old, I take her already for wife.'

'If I ask Paulaine for this girl . . .? – She is not yet married – What would he say?'

'He would say that the boy write already his letter. But who knows? If the boy should say that he does not want the girl, then you can make your arrangement. But . . . it is the daughter of Paulaine, and the boy would not dare to say such words and remain in this village . . . unless it is over a big thing, over a fault of the girl. And in such a girl, schoolmaster, it is very hard to find fault.'

'The boy could be made not to want the girl,' the schoolmaster said. 'If I had powerful friends, they could arrange this wedding for me.'

Dardain opened his eyes wide. He spoke quietly.

'I think you are serious, schoolmaster. But you ask very much. You do not know how much you ask for.'

'I have done many things for Kumaca. I have done much for my friends. Now I need something. And my friends . . . Do they help me?'

'Too much. It is too much what you need,' Dardain said, fear edging his voice.

'No,' the schoolmaster said. 'They don't help. They say it is too much. Always when a man wants something that is a little difficult, they say it is too much. If I said to Paulaine, for a sum, I ask you to break the engagement with the boy . . .?'

'Do not make that talk with Paulaine,' Dardain said sharply.

'Why not to speak to Paulaine?'

'I know the man. Do not make such talk with him. Perhaps you can speak to the boy. And for a sum . . . maybe. But he is young, and does not know life. He thinks about love, and what wonderful thing it is. Better speak to his father. Francis Assivero is in much debt, and for a price, maybe he will persuade the boy to give up the girl. But then he will want a reason why his son should give up the girl. Do you have such a reason to give him?'

'Tell him that the schoolmaster wants her. That is reason enough.'

'With love, schoolmaster, that is not reason enough.'

'Love, Dardain! What is it you talk about love?'

Dardain said, 'For me, love is something in the imagination. With the young people, the imagination and what is real come very close together and mix, so they think they feel what love is.'

The schoolmaster pierced Dardain with his eyes. His tone was a little loud, and aggressive.

'Tell Assivero that the girl is with child by another,' he said.

'And what will Paulaine say to that?'

'He must not tell Paulaine. He must not tell anyone. It is a reason only for his ears, so that he may persuade his son to give up the girl.'

'You are crazy, schoolmaster. Who shall I say make this girl with child?'

'Do you have to say that?'

'He will want to know. For the sake of his feelings.'

'I want the girl, Dardain,' the schoolmaster said.

'I do not think you want her, *bouge*.'

128

The schoolmaster took up the bottle with the rum.

'Why you say that?'

'Let us take another drink and I will tell you. Pour first.'

The schoolmaster poured his drink, then Dardain took the bottle. They drank. The schoolmaster was looking at Dardain. Dardain played with the empty glass in his hands.

'*Bouge*, you say I am your friend? Eh?'

'Yes.'

'And you say I have intelligence?'

'Yes,' the schoolmaster said. 'You are intelligent.'

'Yee-s but you treat me like a child. Why is this? Eh? Why don't you tell me why among all the women in Kumaca, you seek to have the most difficult, a girl that is already written for?'

'You wrong me, Dardain. Haven't I told you of my needs, and of the thoughts in my mind, and the feelings in my body?'

'But you do not say why you want this girl above all others. Luciana has the juiciest breasts a man can dream of. She is not bad to look at, and I myself have tasted her cooking.'

The schoolmaster said: 'I want the girl. That is all I can tell.'

'That is not enough. If the boy did not write the letter, yes. But he write the letter, and more must be said.'

'Dardain, I ask you to go to Paulaine and tell him I would like his daughter for wife.'

'And what will I say to him when he tells that she is already written for? Eh?' Dardain pleaded. 'Eh? Tell me in reason, Eh?'

'You will tell him I need her.'

'Yes. And he will say that the son of Assivero needs her, and what is more has written a letter. And he has sent him already his reply. Such a thing could cause a war between the families of Kumaca, Mr Schoolmaster.'

'You will tell him that my need is greater than that of the boy. You will speak to him about the road that I have caused to be built, and of my loneliness. And of the children I teach at the school. And you will say that if I do not have the girl for wife, I cannot continue in Kumaca, that I must leave.'

'I can see that you do not know this Paulaine, schoolmaster. But you are my friend and have helped me, and I will put up my reluctance and will speak to Paulaine Dandrade. It will cost you something, schoolmaster, for it is a bargain I will have to make with him. I do not know if it will succeed. I will try.'

'I will pay. Let it succeed. You will get me this girl.'

'Then I will see Francis Assivero. When he speak to his son, then I myself will go to Paulaine. It will be better that way.'

'Do you think that Assivero will agree?'

'His mind is big, but he owes too much in my shop to refuse me.'

'You make me feel again that I have a friend, Dardain. Let us take another drink.'

They had a drink.

Dardain said, 'Tell me, is the girl really with child?'

'Promise not to ask more questions,' the schoolmaster said after a long silence.

'I make the promise.'

'And tell this to no one, only Assivero if he needs a reason. The priest is coming very soon, and if we are quick, he can do the ceremony.'

'I make the promise.'

The schoolmaster's voice was hoarse.

'She is with child.'

'Who make her with child?' Dardain asked, leaning forward.

'No more questions,' the schoolmaster said sharply.

'Good. I do not ask them. But I advise, better leave alone this girl. Leave alone this idea'

'I cannot,' the schoolmaster said. 'I cannot.'

'I do not ask any more,' Dardain said. 'Not any more.'

Chapter Eleven

I

Francis Assivero was a very sensitive man and he did not much like Dardain the shopkeeper, because in his presence he felt less than a man. This was so not only because he was heavily indebted to Dardain, but because the shopkeeper would choose any occasion to humiliate him over his indebtness, regardless of who was present. If he protested, something which his own pride rarely allowed him to do, Dardain would become aggressively apologetic and ask him if he couldn't take a joke. He could take a joke, yes. But he didn't appreciate Dardain's idea of a joke. But he couldn't do better. It was the only shop. So he continued to drink his rum there, and take goods for his home, on credit, paying whenever he could from proceeds of his cocoa crop, or with the money he got from working with Consantine Patron. It hurt him to be indebted, and it hurt him more to continue to credit. He could still remember the day when this Dardain, a thin, little man with two teeth missing, limped into Kumaca with nothing – nothing but his bruised face and a paper bag, and the only thing he had then was a grin which made you take pity on him, which now with time and his big prosperity had disappeared along with the bruises on his face and the paper bag. In those days, he Francis Assivero was the man owning perhaps half of Kumaca. But then the cocks started to lose the battles in the gayelle, and he started to bet more heavily. So things moved down, slipped down. Most of the land went, and the cocks went. And now he had to go to the shop of this son-of-a-bitch Dardain to ask for something and have it put in a book.

Francis Assivero could write his name; he had never learned to read. So even in the old days, when Dardain put something in the book, it was put, and he didn't know what it was. And he didn't ask to see the book because he was not overkeen to make an ass of himself knowing full well that he could not read. In the days before when old Johnny had the shop, Johnny would say, you have so much, and he would pay so much, but now the only way to know how big was his debt was Dardain telling him, 'She getting fat, you know.' And to this he would answer even as he answered Johnny in the old days: 'Well, you will have to take the land.' But where in those days he had so much land and money was coming in from his cocoa, those words were a joke which Johnny knew; now that he had hardly any land (in fact, no land, for what remained he had pledged in his mind to his two remaining sons), he said the words with little of their earlier meaning, but rather with a half-resigned face saving apprehension and irony. He had no intention of surrendering that land. In truth, Assivero did not like to go to the shop of Dardain now. Whenever he had to, he tried to efface himself with a silence and a humility that only a man who knew what pride was could realize.

Now this night, Francis Assivero left home to go to the forest to hunt. But he wanted some batteries for his torchlight, and some carbide to put in the pan for his headlight. He had to go to the shop first. Dark clouds ruffled the sky. It was going to be cold that night.

The shop of Dardain, at that hour, held a few people. On one side of the wooden screen, women were getting provisions for the night or for the morning, on the other side of the screen a few men were talking over a flask of rum. Francis Assivero went over to the side with the men. He called out to them, but made no attempt to join them. He stood in a corner by himself, and waited for Dardain to come to serve him. He was thinking now of the tracks he had seen in the forest. It was a lappe. He would wait for it tonight. He had already that day built his scaffold in the crook of a young crappo tree, where he would sit and wait for the animal.

Dardain came over to serve him.

'Ah, *bouge*,' Dardain said. 'Like you going to hunt.'

Although Francis Assivero was far from the man that he used to be, there was about him something which still commanded respect, a sort of uneasy dignity.

'Why for you call me *bouge, bouge*? Look at me. Nothing I have, but you calling me *bouge*. You make a joke of me.'

'How do I make joke of you, Assivero? You look prosperous, with your gun over your shoulder, and your headlight. And though your jacket is old it fits you well. You are going to hunt?'

'I going to sentry a lappe.'

'Alone?'

'Yes. Me one. You want to come? You so will enjoy it better with the dogs. Tonight I do not carry the dogs. But when you ready, tell me, and we will go with the dogs for a 'gouti hunt. There is nothing with more thrills than to hunt 'gouti, if you have the dogs that can run.'

'I do not care for snakes in the bush,' Dardain said.

'Snake is nothing. Look – I have my medicine here in a bottle. Snake bite you, and you drink some of this, and in no time you will poke up all the poison. But I know you like the dry of the shop.'

'You are correct. What you taking?' Dardain said.

'I want some cartridges.'

'On the book? She is getting fat, you know. Very fat.'

'Soon she will make baby, then? Bring the book. And I want cigarettes and a nip of rum for this cold night.'

'How much cigarette?'

'Give me two pack.'

Dardain brought the articles, and put them on the counter before Assivero. Then he went back for the book on which Assivero's name was written. He returned with the book and stood behind the counter and screwed up his face.

'Hmm,' Dardain muttered, looking into the book. 'Hmm!'

Francis Assivero put the cartridges, one pack of cigarettes, and the rum in the pockets of his jacket. He opened the other pack of cigarettes and, about to light one, he shook the box of matches which he was using.

'Bring two box of matches. Ah, and I know I forget something. I want some batteries and a quarter pound of carbide for this headlight.'

'How much batteries you want?'

'Bring three. That is all.'

Dardain creased his forehead and grunted, 'Hmmm!'

When he resumed with the matches and the other articles, he said, 'We have to talk, you know. This thing getting over too fat. It will bust, man.'

Francis Assivero grinned despite himself.

'I don't understand how it get so fat so quick. Is only two months since I bring in the cocoa, and is you self that take out your share, and give me the balance of the money. You give almost nothing. And since then, I bring for you a deer and two lappe.'

'She was already very fat,' Dardain said. 'And every day you drink. It adds up.'

'I must stop drinking,' Assivero said seriously.

'I do not say that. I know you must have your drink. But the account come fat-fat, and then how will you pay? Eh? I squeeze myself to give you something from the cocoa money, because I know how it is with you. I squeezed. But the account was very big. It is still very big.'

'If I cannot pay, then, *bouge*, take the land.'

'I do not want to take your land, Assivero. But we will have to talk.'

Assivero said, 'And last year, you self know how my crop was bad.'

'I know, yes. But when I go to the grocery in Zanilla, I cannot tell them about your cocoa crop. I must take out my money. It is very hard. And then I hear your son is to be married. And that is another story I want to talk to you about.'

Assivero broke the neck of the cigarette he was smoking, stubbed out the lighted end, and put the other section into the half-empty matchbox.

He said, 'We cannot talk here.'

'I know you do not like to make your affairs the business of the public,' Dardain said.

'I going to hunt tonight.'

'You must go?'

'I know where the lappe is passing. I should be in the forest already,' Assivero said.

'I do not want to keep you back. But we must talk.'

'When I come back from the forest, eh?'

'Yes. Go and shoot your lappe first. But do not forget. Good, eh?'

'Good.'

Dardain looked again at the book on which the account of Assivero was written.

'Man, she is very big. She is too big. I would not like to stop your madame from taking things. We have to talk,' Dardain said, shaking his head sadly.

Francis Assivero looked at Dardain. His voice deepened.

'You better talk to me tonight, Dardain. I will see about the lappe tomorrow. Or I will go late and headlight in the forest for manicou.'

'No. Go and make your hunt. Tomorrow when you come back.'

'I do not like how you talk, Dardain. It is not good the way you talk.'

'I just tell you, Assivero. But tomorrow I will see you. We talk better.'

'All right. I just tell you I do not like the way you talk.'

Francis Assivero went out of the shop. As he walked into the night, he felt in his pocket for the nip, took it out, uncorked it and had a drink.

That Dardain. He did not like that Dardain. He did not like the way he talked. What did he mean about stopping his madame from taking things? Ah, that man was a scamp, a damn thief. But how will I know about my account, I never learned to read. Well, he will have to take the land, he thought, in habitual consolation. Let him take it.

II

Francis Assivero did not shoot the lappe that night. He sat on the scaffold he had built on the crappo tree, and listened above the night noises to the animal come trip trip trip over the dead leaves, and he waited for it to come out into the open, from behind the trees; waited. And when he turned the headlight upon it – too soon – it was still behind the trees, and suddenly turning and streaking off deeper into the forest. It didn't make sense wasting a cartridge. Patience was the thing in this type of hunting, and timing. He should have waited longer.

Next evening he was still thinking of the lappe that had escaped him, as he walked to the shop of Dardain. Maybe Dardain had given him bad luck. Maybe it was the talk resting on his mind that had caused him to turn out of time with the animal still behind the trees. He didn't like the kind of talk Dardain made at all.

Assivero went slowly, and when he arrived at the shop, the last customer was just leaving.

'Ah! You come just in time. I just had you in thoughts,' Dardain said.

'I come,' Assivero said.

'Good. Go around by the house. The dogs lock up. I coming in a minute. We will talk inside.'

Francis Assavero went around to the house, and in a little while, Dardain came and let him into a large, unswept room cramped with boxes, crates, and bags for the shop. There was a good kerosene lamp, a table with three legs, two chairs with smoked herring boxes on them, and a hammock tied across the room.

'It good to have a little chat now and then,' Dardain said. 'You see how the place is. Nowhere to sit down. Look – siddown on this box.'

He cleared the box of its load.

'Make yourself comfortable. Let me bring a drink.'

Nowhere in Dardain's tone was a trace of the insinuations of the previous evening. If anything, his attitude suggested an apologetic spirit of welcome, and an anxiety to please. This, translated to his own terms, did not escape Assivero.

Dardain returned with a bottle of rum and two glasses which he placed on a section of a box near the one on which Assivero was seated. He himself would sit in the hammock. He indicated the bottle to Assivero.

'Let us fire one.'

Assivero looked suspiciously at the bottle.

Dardain uncorked the bottle.

'Come, Assivero, take a drink,' he said, holding out the bottle to the other man.

Assivero took the bottle and poured himself a drink.

Dardain was saying: 'I really want a woman in this place bad. Can't invite people in place like this. I don't have time even to sweep.'

'You don't want no woman here,' Assivero said. 'What you want woman here for when you getting so much outside?'

Dardain smiled complacently.

'No. I really want a woman here. But maybe you right . . . I get accustom with things crazy about the place.'

He took the bottle and poured himself a drink.

'How was the hunt last night? You shoot the lappe?'

Assivero shook his head.

'But I will shoot it. I going back tomorrow. It still feeding. I don't even make a shot. It was right behind a tree. That save it.'

'Big one?'

'Good size one.'

Assivero put his glass to his head, emptied it. Dardain sipped his own drink, and pushed the bottle nearer to Assivero.

'A good hunter-man like you will catch it.'

'I must catch it.'

Assivero poured another drink and lit a cigarette.

Dardain said, 'I really want to talk to you about your account. Man, she getting heavy in truth. But right now I hear something that more heavy than your account.'

'What could be more heavy than my account?'

'The world have some heavy things,' Dardain said solemnly.

Assivero drew deeply on his cigarette.

'And what is this heavy thing you hear?'

'I don't like what I hearing. Don't like it at all,' Dardain said, shaking his head gravely.

Assivero smoked his cigarette and looked at Dardain.

'You don't hear anything?' Dardain asked. 'I never would believe it, but it comes from good, solid grounds.'

'I do not hear anything,' Assivero said, a little uneasily.

'Where is your son?'

'Which one?'

'The one that is to married.'

'He is in Valencia. He is with the men working on the road.'

Dardain sighed. He shook his head.

'That boy is too young for this thing to happen in his life. He is too young.'

'For what thing to happen?' Assivero asked.

'I mean the girl he is to married,' Dardain said.

'There is not a better girl in the whole of Kumaca and in Valencia too,' Assivero said. 'What wrong with she?'

'It is bad what I hear. You mean you really do not hear anything?'

Assivero looked at the bottle, like he wanted to drink, then he looked for a place to put the spent cigarette butt. He did not see any place, and he stubbed it out on the cover of the matchbox. He took out another cigarette, and began tapping it against the matchbox.

'I don't hear anything,' he said.

'I am not the one to tell you this at all. But you hear these things – It is a big surprise . . . Where is the boy now? . . . Oh, yes, you tell me already. He down Valencia working on the road. It is little easier so. Not much easier. Take a drink and hand me the bottle quick.'

They had the drinks.

'For the boy own good,' Dardain said in a very grave and sombre tone, 'you have to mash this thing up. I know the kind of man you is and so I advise you. I do not think Paulaine self know. And with the mind Paulaine have, you must do it careful.'

'Mash up what? You not talking about the wedding? Dardain, you crazy.'

Francis Assivero wanted to lean back and observe Dardain carefully, but there was no support for his back. He leaned forward instead.

'Dardain, my son write a letter for the girl. I go with Consantine Patron and carry the letter. The answer come back. They agree. They young. They could make a living together. Why now you tell me I must mash up the wedding? They find the girl in fault? Eh?'

Dardain got out of the hammock, and paced across the room.

'That is why I didn't want to tell you anything . . . But I done put myself in it. I will tell you. But you have to keep cool. You have to hold it a secret from everybody – even from Paulaine.'

'You talk all the time in riddles. Tell me this thing, Dardain.'

'You have eyes? You could see?' Dardain asked.

'Tell me this thing,' Assivero said.

'I tell you to take a good look at the girl. Take a good look.'

Francis Assivero smiled and poured himself a drink. He drank slowly, and was smiling still.

'Suppose is Pedro? Suppose is the boy self do the job? Eh?'

Dardain went back to the hammock.

'Is not the boy.'

'What you mean, is not the boy? Is you, then?'

'Is not your son.'

'You not talking sense, Dardain. You talk all the time and you tell me nothing.'

'I tell you, you will have to take back the letter. And for the boy own good, mash up the business. That is what I telling you.'

'But how can you know is not the boy who do the job? . . . But you make all this talk.'

Dardain said: 'If I was *cullion*, fool, Assivero, you feel I make this talk with you? I know what I say. Watch if you have eyes in your head. Watch the girl.'

'Dardain, you talking stupid, man. Who else could do the job if is not Pedro? I make child when I had eighteen years,' Assivero said, taking two quick puffs on his cigarette.

'But I tell you, Assivero. People have their eyes on that girl a long time. Is not only Pedro does carry something between his legs.'

Assivero was silent for a while, and his face was puzzled.

He said, 'We can talk. But if anybody is to say about mashing up the wedding, is Pedro self. Or the girl. I don't have nothing to do with that.'

'And let him mind another man child? And when time come he kill her dead and get in big trouble? Use your sense, Assivero. Why you think I talk to you?'

Assivero looked around like a cornered deer.

'How Paulaine don't know about this?' Assivero asked in a low tone, not so sure of himself now.

'Pauline not looking for that. How will he know? When last you see the girl?'

'A long time. And how come you know, Dardain?'

'I have my information.'

Francis Assivero shifted restlessly on the box.

'I sure you not know what you saying, Dardain. You cannot know what you saying.'

Dardain said, 'I ask you not to let Paulaine know of this. It will be too bad if he knows.'

'And if I talk to him, will I not tell him? I cannot just say to the man, I want back the letter of my son. That will be grounds for big trouble. Dardain, I do not like this thing. I find it too hard to believe also.'

'Go and look at the girl.'

'You know what I going to do? I going to tell the boy. Let him do what he thinks. It is his affair.'

You do not like your son, Assivero. How can you tell him such a thing? For him to go mad? Eh? For him to kill the girl? Eh?'

'He must know sometime.'

'I tell you, do it first, then tell him. It will not be so hard for him then. You yourself know how it is when a man is young. Perhaps it is even better he stay where he is. I can get a job for him in Zanilla. He can stay there. But you must mash it up, for his sake.'

Francis Assivero stood up. It was as if he wanted to run. He couldn't run. The veins stood out on his temple.

'You do not think he will want to come and see the girl? He has the blood of Assivero in him.'

'So you prefer he get into trouble? Maybe kill? Maybe go mad, eh?'

'It is his *affaire*. I do not interfere yet. Let us talk now of this account I have for you. This news does not feel good inside of me. I want to go outside.'

'You better sit down, Assivero, I know it is a not nice thing for your son. That is why I say for you to do it on your own. Do not say anything to the boy. Only let it be known to Paulaine Dandrade, and do not make too great a fuss over the affair. It will soon be forgotten. And everything will be all right again.'

'No, Dardain. It is the affair of my son. I have made mess enough of my own affairs. I do not think I will tell him even. Let us see this account now, and then I go.'

Dardain stirred in the hammock, and his voice was low now, and his tone now was the same as it was the evening before – menacing.

'Assivero, you do not understand. *I ask you to do this for me.*

'Why you ask me? Is you who breed the girl?'

'We are not talking about that. Look – I better bring your account book. We will talk better with it.'

140

'Bring it,' Assivero said, in a small voice, watching with his eyes as Dardain got out of the hammock and went out of the room.

Dardain returned with the book, turned up the lamp, and showed the book to Assivero, although he knew that he could not read.

'See how fat it is? And you did not have much cocoa this year. How will you pay? Maybe I have to take over the lands. Eh? I do not want to take your lands, Assivero. But if you cannot pay, I will have to do it.'

'So you take my lands for your money, eh, Dardain? How much is the account, you do not say.'

'Almost five hundred dollars. You owe me four hundred and seventy-seven dollars and some cents. It is a lot of money, Assivero. You hardly have any cocoa to depend on. Look at the book yourself. Where will I get my money? And every day you drink in my shop.'

'It is a lot of money, yes.' Assivero said very softly.

He felt weak. Already he had lost so much, given up so much land. What would he leave for his sons? It was bad for a man not to leave something for his sons. You are not a father then. And where would Pedro build his house? And what about Robert who was sick with this sickness that the bushbaths of Mama Cici could not cure, nor the rubbings of Rudolpho and Papa Marcelle?

'We have to talk about the land,' Dardain said.

'I will talk about it,' Assivero said. 'But not now. Tomorrow, please.'

'We talk now,' Dardain said, striking a closed fist into his palm.

'You say we talk now. Good, we talk now,' Assivero said weakly, swallowing spittle.

'Look, man, if you will do what I ask, I forget what you owe me.'

'You mean with my son?'

Dardain nodded.

'I cannot meddle in the affair of my son.'

'It is also your affair. It is your name the boy carries. I tell you the truth.'

'You have too great an interest in this matter, Dardain. Why?'

'Let us say that I have an interest. You will do what I ask?'

'What it is you want me to do?' Assivero said tiredly.

'Go first in secret and see for yourself and satisfy yourself with the condition of the girl, and do not tell anybody. Then do what I tell. Go to Paulaine and say that the wedding is off. For your own pride and for his, do not make much of a fuss.'

'No, I do not do this. Paulaine will want to know why.'

'I will take care of that. There will not be much fuss. I will talk to Paulaine. Your boy is young. In a little while he will forget. You will do that, eh? When you do that I will cross the whole account from off the book.'

'You make me sell my son, Dardain?'

'I make a bargain with you. It is for your benefit. And do not tell me that you are the man who wants for his son to married a girl with child for another in her belly. You will do it, Assivero?'

'Dardain, you squeeze my stones. Why you do this?'

Assivero panted there on the box, then took out his handkerchief and wiped his forehead.

'If she is not with child, do not do it, Assivero. But I know she is with child . . . so . . .'

'I will go and see the girl,' Assivero said, making to stand, but not standing, held by Dardain's eyes and his words now.

'In secret, remember. Do not even tell your wife.'

'I will first see the girl.'

'And when you talk to Paulaine and settle the matter, come back, and I will cross out the account from the book. I will not have to take your land again.'

Francis Assivero sat tiredly on the box, his small frame swaying, his eyes looking absently at the bottle not yet finished on the other box. Dardain tapped the account book to draw his attention.

'You will have one for the road, eh?'

Assivero looked at the bottle, then he took it up, uncorked it. He poured a drink, and gazed at the liquid in the glass. He looked at Dardain.

'Why you do this to me, Dardain? Eh?'

'I do you nothing, Assivero. I do you a favour.'

'A favour, eh?'

Dardain poured himself a drink. Assivero looked at the rum in his own glass, put it to his head and emptied it. He got to his feet.

'Tomorrow, eh?' Dardain said.

Assivero did not say anything.

'Tomorrow, eh, Assivero. It will not be hard to do.'

'When is the priest coming to Kumaca?' Assivero asked.

'The day after tomorrow. You want to see him special?'

'Yes. I have to make a confession.'

'What is your confession?'

Assivero looked fixedly at Dardain.

'I have in my heart and in my body a great heat to shoot two men. And I am afraid that I do it. So I will make the confession before the feeling takes hold of me.'

Dardain laughed nervously.

'Who are these two men?'

'One of them is me. You can guess the other one for yourself,' Assivero said tensely.

'Of course, you do not mean that, Assivero. You cannot.'

Assivero did not say anything. He walked to the door.

'Tomorrow, eh, Assivero,' Dardain said.

But the father of Pedro did not answer.

Chapter Twelve

I

Woot-woot, woot-woot were the sounds the king-of-the-woods made now in the quiet forest behind the schoolhouse. Woot-woot, woot-woot; grey ugly, doleful sounds, conjuring in the still and unpeopled evening, visions of the eerie and supernatural. Woot-woot, woot-woot.

The schoolmaster was sitting on his gallery, and he listened a while to the bird, and thought that its notes sounded as a direct and personal warning to him; and he wondered whether he had been wise in confiding in Dardain, and would Francis Assivero handle the matter entrusted to him with the tact which was so necessary?

Woot-woot, the bird called again, and the schoolmaster raised his eyes above the forest to the blue sky where sparse white clouds drifted, bringing into being transient pieces of cloud-sculpture of every-changing shapes. They looked like islands. Islands had so many different shapes. Looking at these islands now, he thought of the places he had never been to, had seen only in atlases. To his ears came the low, clear warning of the king-of-the-woods, and he wondered whether it wouldn't be better for him to leave Kumaca, ride out on his white horse, and be gone. But in the sky now he identified an 'island'. The Rock of Gibraltar, it was. And embracing this as another and more cogent sign now, he knew that he would remain. This was his world. It was no mere inclination to remain, it was a duty. If he left, what would become of the villagers, the council, the school, the road, the many projects that he had in his brain. It was a duty. He would not run away. The girl was pleasant in her way, too, and she could make him a wife. Certainly there would be little complications, but there were always complications.

The schoolmaster felt that things would be ironed out. They must be. This village was his. And he felt now not only as if he had discovered Kumaca, but had had it willed to him by some Sovereign of The Backward Regions. He heard the call of the king-of-the-woods, and looked from the sky to the forest. With some irritation, he said, aloud, 'Why doesn't that bird shut its stupid trap?'

A mile away at his home, Francis Assivero came through the front door. He was dressed to hunt, and although it was early, carried his headlight around his head. That, the poniard case hanging at his side, and the shot-gun over his shoulder, made him look small, and everlasting, like a stunted tree that refused to grow or to die. He stood in the yard and checked the cartridges in his pocket – six, and saw that he had cigarettes and matches. Then he whistled the dogs. He had three dogs. Two only appeared at the first call. He whistled again and heard the third dog rushing through the bushes at the back of the house. He touched the tin with the cigarettes in his pocket, and restrained himself. He would have his coffee first. And he had almost forgotten the bake his wife was preparing for him. He sat down in the yard to wait. It was still early. No rain tonight either, he thought, looking at the sky. He thought now of the bargain with Dardain and hated himself. Then he saw his son Robert at the window, looking at him, as if he were seeing what he was thinking.

'What happen to you?' Assivero asked with reflex aggression, retaliating at this intrusion.

'Nothing, Papa.'

The father softened now.

'Your face does not say so.'

Assivero stood up.

'Your foot still hurting you?' he asked the boy.

'It is not worse than yesterday, Papa.'

'And what makes your face so?'

'It is nothing, Papa. I just watch you make ready to hunt.'

'And you feel sorry to see your father, eh?'

'I know you can hunt, Papa.'

Francis Assivero felt very fumbly and awkward. He reached for his cigarettes.

'I would take you. But now you cannot come. One of these days, eh,' he said.

'Pedro says that I will walk better if I go to the doctors in the hospital at Port-of-Spain.'

'It is a far place. But soon I have to take you.'

'I will go to hunt when I am better,' Robert said. 'What will you catch, Papa?'

'A lappe, I hope. I see the moon change, and the lappe will not be feeding at the same place, so I take the dogs.'

'It will be easier with the dogs?'

'No. There will be much running. And if the lappe gets to a river, then it will be ten times harder to catch. But the dogs are good. They will catch him.'

Assivero glanced across at the kitchen and saw his wife at the door.

'I am going,' he said to Robert.

He went to the kitchen and his wife handed him a cup of coffee. When he had taken it, she gave him a bake wrapped in thick brown paper and tied in the cloth, which he put into one of the pockets of his jacket.

'It is good coffee,' he said when he had drunk the coffee.

Her face showed nothing.

He said, 'I am going.'

'You taking the dogs?'

'Yes. The moon change. The lappe will not feed the same place.'

'True,' she said. 'I hope you have luck.'

Francis Assivero said again, 'I am going.'

'Good,' she said.

He turned and went from the kitchen, taking with him a picture of a slim, big-breasted, narrow-hipped woman. She had much patience, this woman. She was too good for him. And he thought, maybe it is better Pedro do not marry so young. And he thought too of the bargain he had made with Dardain. Dusk was some minutes off. He would walk down by Paulaine Dandrade and take a look at the girl. He whistled the dogs again. He thought: Look what you come to, eh, Francis Assivero. Dog! Worse than dog! Worm! Criminal! Nothing! You should shoot yourself.

*

Christiana made supper early that evening, went and sat alone on the fallen log near the cocoa house. She was looking at the small birds swaying the long stems of grass at the edge of the cocoa field, when she heard the parrots squawking. She looked up and watched them crossing in the sky over the forest. She remained, after they had gone, looking at a piece of cloud shaped like a priest. Father Vincent had said that he would pray for her. She had prayed and waited. Prayed and waited. The stiffness was still in her belly, and her breasts were pushing against the cloth of her dress, and even her ankles were getting bigger. These days, she avoided her father, and prayed and waited. Father Vincent said that he would pray for her. And when she had to wash clothes, she went down to the river after the woman had left. It was hard to want to cry and not cry. She wished that she could cry. She wanted to cry, needed to cry. It was hard to want to cry, and not cry. The piece of cloud looked just like a white-gowned priest.

Christiana heard a twig snap behind her, turned and saw her brother Humphy sitting on a stone, looking at her. He was always watching her now. She smiled. He came out of hiding, towards her.

'What are you there hiding, looking at me for?'

'I was watching for the doves,' he said.

She knew that he was not speaking the truth.

'Come, Humphy. What is the matter?'

He came over to her, his head bent, looking down at his bare toes.

'Eh, boy, what is it?'

He kept on looking at his toes.

'Manuel says that maybe you catch a cold,' he said.

'Why he say that?'

'I tell him how you look fat,' the little boy said, raking his toes over the ground.

'You tell him that? When?'

'I tell him so yesterday.'

'And what did he say?' she asked gently.

'He say maybe you catch a cold. But I do not hear you coughing. I was looking to see if you would cough.'

'And did you tell Papa?'

'No, I only ask Manuel. It is a cold, eh, Christiana?'

She looked at his little face, turned up with the question on it. She tried not to cry. He was still asking the question with his eyes.

'It is a cold,' she said. 'Where are the others?'

'They chasing squirrels in the cocoa.'

Go and meet them. It is a cold, soon I get better.'

'I was looking to hear you cough,' he said.

'Hem hem hem hem.' She made the sounds, clearing her throat. 'Look, I cough now. Go and meet the others.'

As the little boy turned to go, Christiana thought, I have prayed and waited. I have waited and prayed.

She got up and looked into the sky. The form of the priest had changed. Yes, it was a pool now. A pool. Her mother was waiting for her on the bank of a pool. The pool in the forest. And now Christiana heard her name being called. Who was calling her name? And where was the voice coming from? Christiana turned and began to walk down the path leading away from the house, hearing above the birds in the near trees in the dusk gathering, the voice coming now from the forest, calling her to the forest and the pool where her mother sat waiting to shelter her in her arms, and to kiss her with her lips. Christiana kept on walking. She was unconscious of everything but the voice calling.

Coming up the path that led up to the house of Paulaine Dandrade, Francis Assivero was a little surprised to see the girl Christiana walking towards him; so surprised in fact that all he could do was mumble a good evening which he was not sure she heard. In the gathering dusk, it was useless looking at her to see if what Dardain had said was true. There was something about her too, a manner of intent, and he thought that she was hurrying to get to the shop before it closed. He couldn't even be sure that she had made reply to his greeting. And confused now, and a little relieved that he did not have to face this great, this terrible moment, he decided that he would bypass Paulaine's place that night, and cut through the forest at the earliest opportunity. He wondered where she was going at this hour. Perhaps the shop. Well, he would try to see her tomorrow.

If Francis Assivero had looked back, he would have seen the girl turn off from the track into the forest. He did not look back. One of the dogs began to bark, and he hurried up to it to see if it was on the trail of a wild animal.

II

In Valencia now, Pedro was sitting on the steps of the house in which he camped with some of the men working on the road. He had received his first fortnight's pay this afternoon, and had planned to go to the pictures at Zanilla. He had even got dressed, but when the jeep came, he told the fellows that he wasn't feeling to go again. He had changed his mind. He sat down right there on the steps after they had gone. It was a clear night with many stars and a very thin slice of moon in the sky. Under the house opposite, the men were gambling. Pedro didn't know how to play whappie, and anyway, his money was for another purpose. Except for the fellows gambling under the house across the road, almost everyone had gone out of camp. Those who hadn't gone to the pictures at Zanilla were in the rum-shops in the village, or had taken a girl for a walk somewhere, and Pedro had heard three or four fellows talking about a house where they could get some women.

Pedro didn't feel good. He felt excited. He felt that something was happening. He wanted to go home to Kumaca. He would be off, after working half-day next day and would be free to go home, but he wanted to see Christiana now. He couldn't understand himself. He knew only that there was a powerful feeling of anxiety over him. Always since leaving Kumac, whenever he was alone and thinking of Christiana, he had this sort of feeling. But this evening it was stronger and more pressing than it had ever been.

Pedro sat there on the steps, and he felt that he was being childish and perhaps foolish, but he wanted to go home. He wanted to see Christiana. That very moment. And now he recalled again that she had wanted to tell him something, that time when he had been saying goodbye to her. What was it? He wanted to see her this very moment.

Pedro got up suddenly. He wanted to see the foreman. He wanted to go home at that very moment. He didn't care whether or not it sounded foolish. He wanted to go home. Pedro walked over to the other house across the road where the men were gambling. He did not see the foreman. One of the fellows told him that he would find him down at the village, perhaps in the rum-shop.

'What you want him for?' the fellow asked as an afterthought.

'I want to go home,' Pedro said.

The fellow looked at him. He was so surprised that he didn't laugh even.

Both rum-shops were closed when he got to them. At the second one, the Chinese shopkeeper was selling at the window. He told the shopkeeper that he wanted to see the foreman.

'Who he?' the shopkeeper asked, curtly.

'Mr Dabreau.'

No hav' Babreau here. Go other shop.'

But he had already been at the other shop.

'Please. Dabreau,' Pedro pleaded.

He remained a long time pleading with the shopkeeper, until finally the Chinese man, seeing that he was prepared to remain there the whole night if necessary, went grumbling inside, and called the foreman.

Seeing the foreman now, Pedro felt very foolish, and didn't know how he would explain that he wanted to leave for Kumaca at that same moment.

'What the hell you want?' the foreman asked him.

He was a big hunk of man with a big moustache, and when he smiled, his eyes seemed to want to shoot out of the sockets. He was a little drunk.

'Foreman, I want to go home.'

'You want to go home! This hour! Somebody dead?'

'Nobody dead, foreman.'

'Well, I never hear more shit. Where you living, boy?'

'Kumaca, foreman.'

'Look boy, don't play the arse, you hear. What you wanto go home for?' He looked at his watch.

'Look at the time. Nearly nine o'clock. And Kumaca is eleven miles. Tomorrow. You have half-day tomorrow. What wrong with you?

Why you don't go and see if you could get a pieca ass in the village? What you going home for? Eh?'

'I just want to go home, foreman. I have this feeling . . .'

'Boy, go and getta pieca ass, then go in your bed. Nothing put you to sleep faster. How much years you have?'

'Twenty-one.'

'Young and hot. Look – better go in camp and sleep, you hear. Go on.'

Pedro stood his ground.

The foreman said, 'Never meet such crazy son a bitch.'

At the same moment, two of the surveyors who also worked on the road came out of the rum-shop and came over to the foreman. They were both a bit tight.

'Dabreau, what the hell you out here bullshitting about now?' the tall one with the long nose asked.

The foreman said, 'This boy here wanto go home now! Ever hear more crazy shit?'

'Where's he living?' the same surveyor asked.

'Kumaca,' the foreman said. 'Eleven miles from here! And he going to walk. That distance. This hour! Eh?'

The foreman turned and looked at the surveyors.

He said, 'Ever hear such crazy shit? Nine o'clock in the night.'

Both surveyors looked at Pedro now.

The tall one who had been speaking all the time asked:

'Sure you wanto go home, boy? Sure you don't want to go sleep in some whore-house in Zanilla? Wouldn't like what you'll pick up in a whore-house, you know.'

Pedro said, 'No, sir. I want to go home. I have to go.'

The second surveyor, a large fellow with a big neck, looked at him, then turned to the foreman.

'If he want to go home, why not let him go?'

The foreman looked at the surveyors.

'Yes, let the bloody boy go, if he wants to, eh, Solo,' the big-necked surveyor said.

The foreman glared at Pedro.

'All right. But you going to lose half-day pay for tomorrow, hear?

And get your arse back here Monday morning bright and early, if you wanto work.'

'Yes, foreman,' Pedro said, nodding thankful and apologetically all around.

'All right,' the foreman said.

'Thanks, sir,' Pedro said, starting up the street, running.

The foreman was saying: 'We really have some crazy bitches working on this gang.'

But Pedro was already up the road. And then he was on the track to Kumaca.

Pedro ran, his heart pounding, through the weird shadows of the trees in the weak moonlight, smelling the forest smell, hearing the doleful notes of the poll-poll singing out suddenly, or flying up, startling him at the last moment of his approach, and the frog voices, and the long shrill, piercing screams of the cigales, and the noises the wind made with the trees. Ran, forgetting his fright, then suddenly remembering it, and running faster despite his panting and his tired thigh muscles.

Then he was thinking how foolish it would appear, him bursting into Kumaca's quiet at this late hour. And if everything was all right, what would he say? What reason would he give for his impatience and his haste? But despite these thoughts, he ran on, knowing that he had to get to Kumaca, not really knowing why, but knowing with a primitive, instinctive certainty that he had to get there. But would he see Christiana? Could he go running to her father's house and ask at that hour for her? And when he saw her, what would he say? If he saw her, what would he say? Suddenly, Pedro thought that it was all very foolish of him, and that he might have done better to have gone with the other fellows to the pictures at Zanilla. But still, he wanted to get to Kumaca, and he was drawing nearer and nearer.

III

Paulaine Dandrade had grown increasingly worried as the night progressed and he did not see his daughter. Even if she had gone to

152

the shop, it was time for her to return. And she hardly would go to visit Robert, the brother of Pedro, without saying where she was going.

Paulaine put on his tall rubber boots and his hat, snatched up his shot-gun, and torchlight, and hurried out into the night. He inquired first at the shop, then at the home of Francis Assivero where he thought she might have gone to see Robert who was ill. He walked all over the village, making inquiries. He did not see her. He did not meet anyone who had seen her. It was late now, and he was suddenly very afraid. It was not at all like Christiana. He was very worried now, and did not know where again to look. He walked aimlessly for a time, shining his torchlight on every suspicious shadow, and starting at any hopeful sound. Something had happened to Christiana.

He was sure of it. Why else would she not be home?

Paulaine went to the house of the schoolmaster now, and knocked on the door. He had a suspicion and a hope. He waited, and knocked on the door again. He knocked for the third time, then he heard someone coming to the door.

'Who is it?' the schoolmaster asked from behind the closed door.

'It is I, Paulaine Dandrade.'

There was no answer from inside the house now, then he spoke again.

It is Paulaine Dandrade here.'

'What do you want?'

'If you will open the door, I wish to speak to you.'

'It is very late. What do you want to speak to me about?'

'I want you to help me. I am sorry to wake you. But I cannot find my daughter Christiana,' he cried.

'She is not here.'

'I do not say she is here. I want to speak with you.'

'Give me a moment, then.'

'Paulaine waited there while the schoolmaster lit the lamp. Then the door was opened, cautiously, and the schoolmaster stood looking down from the steps at him.

'I am looking for Christiana. Since evening I do not see her. I search the whole village, and I do not see her. I ask everybody and they do not see her.'

'I have not seen her,' the schoolmaster said.

'I cannot think what happened to Christiana. I do not know where else to look.'

'I have not seen her.'

'I would look in the forest, but what would she be doing in the forest alone at this hour?'

'It is near midnight,' the schoolmaster said. 'Where do you think she could be?'

'I think she is going to Valencia to meet Pedro who she is to marry. That is all I can think. I must look for her. I must find Christiana. Schoolmaster, you have a horse. Will you ride along the road to Valencia and see if she is walking there?'

'You believe that she has gone to meet this boy?'

'It is all I can think. There or in the forest. But what will she be doing in the forest at this hour?'

'Maybe she get lost in the forest.'

Paulaine shook his head.

'That could be. But I prefer to think that she is walking on the road to Valencia to see this boy who she is to marry. With young girls, there are sometimes many foolish thoughts in the head. You will ride with your horse and see if you find her for me, please?'

'I will try to help you.'

'You will ride, then? I would like to come with you. Your horse can take the two of us.'

'Isn't it better that I go alone? If I find her, where will she ride?'

'When we find her, she will take my place on the horse, and I will walk,' Paulaine said.

'You think she is on the road to Valencia, eh?'

'Where else can she be?'

'Very well. Let me put some clothes on, then I will get the horse.'

'I cannot thank you enough, schoolmaster. Let us go quickly.'

'I will get ready, then saddle the horse.'

The schoolmaster was ready now, and Paulaine got up behind him on the horse.

By accident, the shot-gun which Paulaine was carrying jabbed the schoolmaster in his back.

He asked. 'Do you have to carry your gun?'

'I will be careful with it,' Paulaine said. 'But in the night, I walk very often with it.'

They travelled a little while.

'You think we will find her?'

'We must find her. I cannot understand what get in her head to go away.'

'I hope that you find her, Mr Dandrade.'

'Paulaine sighed deeply.

'Ah!' he said. 'This is a life, eh?'

The schoolmaster did not say anything.

Chapter Thirteen

I

Pedro had been running and was very tired. The sound of his own panting made a great noise in his ears. When he saw the light flashing ahead of him, he just knew that something was wrong. He ran on. The beam of light picked him up, and played over him. And then he stopped, stood panting, before what ever it was.

'Where are you going at this hour, boy?'

It was the voice of the schoolmaster. And as the light dropped to his feet, he could see the schoolmaster on the horse, and Mr Paulaine behind him.

'I am going to Kumaca.'

'You are going to Kumaca. At this hour?' the schoolmaster asked.

'Have you seen my daughter, Christiana?' Mr Paulaine asked.

'She is not on this road,' Pedro said.

'She is not?' the schoolmaster asked.

'Since evening I do not see her,' Paulaine Dandrade said. 'Did she not come to Valencia to see you?'

'I do not see her,' Pedro said.

'You are very late on the road,' the schoolmaster said.

'You say you have not seen Christiana?' Pedro asked. 'You have not seen her. Have you looked for her? Where is she? In the forest, have you searched?' Pedro cried, knowing now that what he had been feeling was true, that something was wrong.

'I thought she was coming to Valencia to see you,' Paulaine said, confusedly.

'And you do not know where she is? How could you let her go away?' Pedro cried. 'We must look for her I must find Christiana!'

Paulaine said, 'We do not know where again to look. I look everywhere already.'

He was very close to tears.

The schoolmaster said, 'Control yourself, Mr Dandrade. If the boy has not seen her, we must go back. You are certain you have not seen her, eh?'

156

Pedro said, 'I am running on this road since night. If she pass here I must see her. She is not on this road, you hear.'

Pedro broke away from them. He started to run.

'I am going to look for her,' he cried.

The schoolmaster said to Paulaine: 'Let us go back.'

Paulaine said, 'The boy ask if I search in the forest. I will search in the forest. I will ring the bell, and wake the people and ask them to go with me and search for her in the forest. I do not understand where Christiana can be!'

The schoolmaster said, 'I hope you find her, Mr Dandrade.'

They rode back to Kumaca, with Pedro running behind the horse. Paulaine jumped off the horse when they reached the schoolyard, and rang the big bell which was rung whenever the priest came, or when there was a death, or some alarm. He rang the bell and he cried out to the villagers to wake up. He rang the bell, and Pedro came up, tired and panting and helped him ring the bell. The schoolmaster went and put his horse in the stable and returned, and they were still ringing the bell, although the villagers were coming out now.

The villagers came out with their night faces, and sleepy eyes, assembled near the schoolyard. Most of the men carried their shotguns. They were all there: Consantine Patron, Dardain, Miguel the great one with the cocks, and Sibley, and the brothers Pampoon, Santo and Ramon, and Martin and Felix Assivero the cousins of Francis Assivero, and Landeau, and a few of the women.

Paulaine said, 'I have not found my daughter. Since evening she is gone. I look everywhere. I have just this moment resumed from the road to Valencia with the schoolmaster, and I do not see her. I think maybe she is lost in the forest. I ask you to help me look for her in the forest.'

They were all very sympathetic and eager to start the search.

'Let us go now,' Consantine Patron said. 'It is late already.'

The schoolmaster came forward now, assumed the authority.

'It is better for us to divide in groups. You, Consantine Patron, take some men, and you, Mr Dandrade take some, and let Landeau take the remaining group.'

'Yes, schoolmaster,' Paulaine said, and started calling the names of some of the men to join him.

'You come with my group, Mr Schoolmaster,' Consantine Patron said.

They remained some time dividing themselves into groups, then they were ready to leave.

Consantine Patron was first to spot the light. It was the headlamp of a hunter moving among the trees, coming towards the school.

'Look!' Consantine said, drawing the attention of the others.

In the grey dawn-light now it was very silent, and even the trees seemed to hold their breaths. The mist unclinging from treetops and curling skywards seemed to freeze and wait. All eyes turned towards the light coming between the trees, moving jerkily to the path. No one drew his breath. They waited and watched.

It was a short man carrying an animal on his shoulder. As he came on to the path, they saw in the light it was Francis Assivero. They watched him come on jerkily, the dogs running at his feet, his poniard case dangling at his side, his shot-gun uncomfortably over the free shoulder, his hat a little askew because with the burden he had to carry he couldn't reach up and fix it. But that was no deer on his shoulder! They watched him come right up to the edge of the group which had without movement or whisper formed into a semi-circle. He faced them. Nobody said a word. Nobody stepped forward to help him. They watched him, and did not breathe, as he ease the body (it was a body) off his shoulder, on to the ground. He straightened up. He looked at them, and his sigh sounded all over Kumaca. He took off his hat, and removed the headlamp, then replaced his hat. He took his shot-gun and leaned on it. His voice was a whisper, very hoarse.

'She was sticking in the bamboo roots in the big river,' he said.

Without being seen to move, Paulaine Dandrade was at the side of the body, with his shot-gun and his grief, not looking at it yet, looking still at Francis Assivero who was feeling in the pocket of his jacket for the tin in which he kept his cigarettes and matches.

'Christiana! Dead?' Paulaine asked weakly, the words sucking in the silence, clutching it to them, becoming heavy, and long, and taking years in the speaking.

'Drowned,' old Assivero said.

In the great silence, nobody moved. Nobody tried to get nearer to

158

have a better look. Paulaine bent his head and shook it the way a wet dog shakes his ears.

Then Pedro moved, stood now next to the body, with his town clothes and the new shoes with which he had run the eleven miles from Valencia in three and a quarter hours, and his back wet with perspiration that had not yet had time to dry.

'Christiana!' he whispered. 'You are dead, Christiana?'

He sank to his knees, on the seams of the new pants he had bought in Zanilla. He took one of her hands, lifted it and put it to his lips. He kissed the hand, then let it go, watched it fall.

'Dead? Christiana?' he cried, taking the hand again, lifting it, letting it go, and watching how it fell, lifelessly, lifeless. He pressed his face to the wet body, and his shoulders were heaving now, and the heavy, tearing sounds escaped him, then he lifted his head and screamed, then put his head back upon the body, his shoulders shaking, heaving, trembling, the sounds twisting through him to his lips.

'My daughter is dead,' Paulaine Dandrade said, as if he were a priest reading something out of the Bible. 'Why is my daughter dead?'

And all the time, Pedro kneeling there, his shoulders heaving, the thick noise of grief twisting through his nostrils and bared teeth, being watched by the stunned, silent villagers; and the trees silent too, and the mist twisting away skywards.

'Why do you walk so far in the forest, my daughter?Eh? Can you tell why she walk so far to die, to drown in the big river, in the deep pool?' Paulaine asked, as a priest on Good Friday with all the sad faces and black garments around him.

'Do you know why my daughter do this thing?' he asked the silent, stony-faced villagers and the trees in the pre-dawn.

Dardain came forward.

He said 'Let us take the body to the house of Paulaine.'

Miguel the great one with the cocks came forward, as did Landeau.

'Her body is swollen already,' Miguel the great one with the cocks said.

'It is the water she drink,' Dardain said. 'Come, let us carry the body to the place of Paulaine, then we go home. The morning is coming up.'

But Pedro still lay sobbing on the body, and Paulaine stood with his shot-gun and his sad face, looking at his dead daughter.

Francis Assivero spoke slowly, and to no one.

'My dogs chase a lappe. They run it to the river. She is there lying in the water between the roots of the bamboos.'

'Let us take up the body,' Dardain said.

But they were listening to Assivero.

'I see her this evening when she was going to the shop of Dardain. I was going to speak with her, but the dusk was falling and she was very busy. I did not stop her. Why, I do not know.'

'You are mistaken, Assivero, she did not come to my shop this evening,' Dardain said.

'Maybe she was going somewhere else. She was going very fast, and I did not stop her.'

'My daughter is dead,' Paulaine said. 'But I do not know why she is dead.'

'It is sad,' Dardain said. 'She was a fine girt Your grief is great, but let us take the body to your place before the sun comes up on it.'

'Your grief is very great,' Paulaine said, as a child repeating after the teacher, or as someone repeating the prayers at the direction of the priest in the confessional. 'Take her, then, and carry her home. I cannot touch her.'

'Come, Miguel! Come, Landeau!' Dardain said. And looking from the men to the body, he said, 'Come, Pedro. It is sad, but we must take her up now.'

Pedro turned from the body, and through his teeth and grimace, said, 'I was coming to see her. She was trying ... What were you trying to tell me? This you were trying to tell me?' he asked, turning to the body.

'Help up your son, Assivero,' Dardain said. 'The sun is already on the hilltops. It will be all right.'

'It will be all right?' Assivero asked, saying the two meanings to Dardain.

'It will be all right,' Dardain said, nodding his head to satisfy Assivero that he had caught both meanings. 'Help up your son now.

The men stood ready to lift the body of Christiana. The villagers now began talking among themselves, ready to move off. Francis Assivero made a step forward, then he stopped.

'Leave my son,' Assivero said. 'And let us talk. For it will not be all right. There is more in this matter.'

'There is more in this matter?' Paulaine asked weakly like an old man that is both deaf and forgetful.

Now the people stopped whispering and were listening, and a cock was crowing.

'There is more in this matter,' Assivero said, with his shortness assuming now a quality of dour indestructibility and menace, so much so that silence lingered about his words, and the air was charged now with a tenseness and expectation.

'You speak out of grief for your son, Assivero. But I tell you, it will be all right.'

Dardain tried to get Assivero's eyes, but Assivero looked directly at him, then turned away.

He winked at Assivero, in an attempt to draw him in.

'It is out of my own grief, I speak, Dardain. My own,' Assivero said.

'There is more in this matter, Assivero?' Paulaine asked, weakly, hopefully, as an old man who, though deaf and forgetful, quickens now as his mind lights on a thought, a phrase that brings back his confidence, and kindles his hope.

'What is it?' Consantine Patron asked.

'The girl was with child,' Assivero said with a sort of aggressive gravity.

Heads turned, eyes rested on Pedro. Silence, and they waited.

'She . . .? My daughter . . . was with . . . child?' Paulaine asked.

Assivero turned quickly to his son.

'Was it you, boy?'

'We were not married,' Pedro said.

'Then it was not you, Pedro-boy?' Assivero asked again, triumph and menace sharp in his voice.

'We were not married,' the boy said.

'You say that Christiana was with child. Not for Pedro,' Paulaine said weakly, again the old man unsure of his ability to understand.

Assivero pointed his right index finger.

'He! Dardain will tell you.'

Dardain said, 'Your walk in the forest and the grief of your son have made you mad, Assivero. I do not know what you talk about. Let us take up the body and take it to the place of Paulaine. Assivero, you make a very bad joke,' he said, trying to wink secretly and compliantly at Assivero.

'No,' Assivero said. 'Tell why you call me to your place to make a bargain to call the wedding off. And tell how you know the girl is pregnant. Now she is dead, everybody can look at her.'

'You do not know what you say. Why should I make such talk with you?'

'I am too poor now, Dardain. My fighting cocks are all gone, and there is little land left. Do I now lie like a dog to your face?'

'Your brain is upset, Assivero. Why do you make this talk now when the girl is dead and grief fills the soul of these two men, and of us all?'

'So I lie! And you did not promise me, this miserable bitch myself, to square the account I have at your shop for me to call the wedding off?'

Dardain chuckled nervously.

'Assivero, your mind is not well. If you will not help me with the body, then I am going home.'

Francis Assivero had been holding his shot-gun with one hand, the butt resting on the ground. Now he lifted it, and broke it.

'Dardain,' he said, feeling now with one hand in the pocket of his jacket. 'I have five cartridges here in my pocket. I will now put one in this gun.'

Everybody was quiet now, and the sun was not yet in sight, but the rays speared the eastern sky over the hills. The people behind Dardain moved away quietly like a wind, and he was left standing alone.

A chilly breeze was blowing now as Assivero put the cartridge into the shot-gun.

'Tell me now that I lie, Dardain,' he said in one tone, and in another, he said, 'And tell me who full the belly of the girl my son was to married!'

Dardain looked around and saw that he stood alone.

'You cannot let this man shoot me. You cannot let him do it. You don't see he is crazy.'

'Tell me once again that I am crazy, and I will shoot you, Dardain.'

'But Assivero . . . Why for you want to shoot me?'

Dardain's voice was sad and very hoarse.

'I do not much care to shoot you, but you say I lie. You say I crazy. You say I foolish. I do not know what I am saying. And the girl is dead. She walk into the forest and drowned in the deep pool. She is with child, you tell me. Not for my son, you tell me. Now I want to know for who this child is, for my sake, for Mr Paulaine sake, and for the sake of my son, and for my own pride. I do not care to shoot you. But I will shoot you, Dardain, because you are not a good man, and for my son's grief, and for myself, because I agree yesterday to your bargain, because I am so worm-poor now that you could talk to me. In my days, Dardain, like you could not feed my gamecocks. It is not your fault that I am how I am. But who knows is not your fault? Who knows you not a thief, robbing people because they cannot read what you put down in the account book?

'And today when I see this girl who so nice, and I think that I, Francis Assivero, who did own more than half Kumaca come so low as now to make bargain with like you who come to Kumaca with a paper bag and bruised face, I get dead inside me, and dry, and for that alone I could kill you. And kill myself. So I have much cause to kill you. But now, I want you to talk, so everybody will know, and for my son and for the girl father to hear.'

'Dardain, who make my girl belly full?' Paulaine asked with a sort of innocent and touching amazement.

'I do not know, Paulaine.'

'Dardain, tell me, please, who make my little girl with child?' Paulaine asked, still with amazement, but now with a sort of menace in place of innocence.

Dardain looked around. He could sense the villagers waiting on his answer.

Francis Assivero said, 'I am going to count to three. I am illiterate, and do not know to count more. Then I going to shoot you, Dardain . . . Already, I talk too much . . . One . . .'

Pedro kneeling at the side of the body, said, 'Papa!'

'. . . Two . . .'

Pedro said again, 'Papa? If it is for me, do not shoot him.'

'For myself. For his insult and for my poorness, and his lies,' Assivero said.

And now the short man wearing an old jacket and a hat, lifted the shot-gun to his shoulder, and in the quiet morning with the sunshine like many spears now in the sky over the hills in the east, and the chilly breeze too slight to shake the leaves heavy with dew, and the mist lifting, no one said a word. The faces with the sleep gone out of them, still with the puffiness about the eyes, gazed. The face of Francis Assivero was very stiff now, and like in pain, and he had shot many animals, and was a very good shot. He sighted along the barrel now in the clear silence, and was very alone and very tall. You heard the breath of Dardain the shopkeeper who had come years ago to Kumaca with his bruised face, his smile and a paper bag, whistling through his nostrils. Then Dardain's scream shattered the stillness, and he was swaying as if rooted, like a tree in a storm.

'Do not shoot me. Don't! I will talk. I will talk!'

And there stood Assivero still very much alone, very tall still, his face stiff, sighting still along the barrel of the shot-gun held straight like the extension of a soldier's arm. Then his nostrils twitched, the pain drained slowly from his face, reluctantly almost, and he came to himself and lowered the gun and looked at Dardain, who now had collapsed on to the ground, passing wind in his pants, violently like the explosions of bamboo bursting. His bowels it seemed had collapsed too, and he tossed now in his fear and his faeces, screaming and crying that he would talk.

'Tell about this matter,' Paulaine Dandrade said, when they had quieted down Dardain, convinced him that he was not going to be shot.

Dardain sat on the ground, and looked around quickly in growing terror, then more slowly.

'Where is the schoolmaster?'

But the schoolmaster was not there.

'For what you want the schoolmaster?' Paulaine asked very politely, fingering the stock of his own shot-gun.

'It is the schoolmaster,' Dardain said.

Pedro who had been on the ground at the side of the body, jumped to his feet.

'Where is the schoolmaster?' he asked.

'It is not the schoolmaster,' Paulaine Dandrade said. 'It cannot be the schoolmaster. You lie, Dardain. It is better that you are shot. I myself will shoot you.'

'I swear,' Dardain screamed, rolling on the ground. 'I swear. Look for the schoolmaster. Ask him. Ask him!'

'You lie too much, Dardain,' Paulaine said with much sternness in his voice. 'You must be lying.' With sadness he added, 'I will hate to shoot the schoolmaster.'

'Where is the man?' Miguel the great one with the cocks asked. 'We must find him.'

'He was here,' Landeau said.

'If you are lying, Dardain, I promise myself to shoot you,' Paulaine said.

'I do not lie,' Dardain said. 'Find the schoolmaster.'

'If you are lying, I make you this promise,' Paulaine said. 'Now let us go to the house of the schoolmaster and see if we find him there.'

Until Francis Assivero began accusing Dardain about the girl Christiana, the schoolmaster had been standing next to Consantine Patron, but when the matter grew more serious, and Patron looked for the schoolmaster, he just glimpsed him back off into the crowd. Consantine Patron kept his eyes on him, and when he saw him slip away from the crowd, he slipped quietly behind him, with his flashlight in one hand, and his shot-gun in the other, and keeping well out of sight, had followed him to his house. While the schoolmaster went into the house, he let himself quietly into the stable where the schoolmaster kept his white horse. He had his suspicions. He leaned his shot-gun against the partition, and waited with his flashlight held ready. He did not have to wait long. In a little while he observed the door of the stable being eased open, and from his darkened corner watched the schoolmaster come in, carrying a small bag and his riding whip. He watched him go to a corner and pick up the saddle. Then he switched on the flashlight, played the beam straight on the face of the schoolmaster.

'You are leaving us, Mr Schoolmaster?' Consantine Patron asked in his kindest voice.

'That light! Take it from my eyes,' the schoolmaster said in his ever-composed voice.

'Not going to say goodbye, even?'

'Take that light from my face.'

'I want to see your face. You have a very strong face, and I want to see it.'

'Do not get me angry,' the schoolmaster said. 'What is wrong with you?'

'They are questioning Dardain now. Are you running away and leaving Dardain alone to answer the questions?'

'I am in no mood for your nonsense. Put out that light.'

'I think you know about the girl, schoolmaster.'

'Think what you like, I am not concerned.'

'But you must be concerned. You are the schoolmaster. But tell me this. Are you leaving us? Now?'

'Put that light out. I have to get on with my business. Do you want to get me angry?'

'The people of Kumaca are very patient, schoolmaster. But we get angry too. You have never seen the people of Kumaca angry. Oh, you would not like to see it. It is not something nice to see ... Do you think Dardain will talk?'

'Get out of my way with your nonsense, man.'

'I tell you, schoolmaster. Assivero will love for him not to talk, so he can shoot him. But we do not hear a shot. That means Dardain has talked. Eh, schoolmaster? Do you think he will talk about you?'

'Get out of my way,' the schoolmaster said very quietly. 'I want to put this saddle on my horse. And please remove that light from eyes.'

'So you want to leave now, eh?' Consantine Patron said.

Despite the light, the schoolmaster had crossed quickly, saddle in hand, and was quite near to Consantine Patron now. And now he moved like a flash, tossed the saddle upon Consantine Patron, knocking the flashlight from his hand. He followed him up, butting him the stomach, butting him again. Then he began to use his riding whip. Hitting Patron with it again and again. Then Consantine Patron saw the shot-gun, and the schoolmaster saw the shot-gun. They both made for it. The schoolmaster grabbed it just a second ahead of Consantine, then Patron held it. They wrestled, very quietly, breathing hard, wrestled very manfully, then the schoolmaster who was the heavier had Patron up against the partition. He pushed him back hard, knocked his hold loose from the gun. Then as Consantine made to kick him, he brought the butt of the shot-gun down on his head. Consantine Patron slumped down, the schoolmaster grabbed his horse, took up the bag, forgot his saddle and riding whip. Then he was going through the door of the stable, to come face to face with Paulaine Dandrade, Dardain, and the crowd of people behind them.

'What is this?' the schoolmaster asked sternly.

'We are looking for you, Mr Schoolmaster,' Paulaine answered, almost apologetically.

'What for, Mr Dandrade?'

'My daughter, she is found. She is dead. She was with child, Mr Schoolmaster.'

'I am very sorry that your daughter is dead, Mr Dandrade.'

Paulaine looked sheepishly at Dardain, then faced the schoolmaster.

'They say . . . They say it is you who make her with child,' Paulaine said.

The schoolmaster looked at Dardain. He did not say anything.

'Is it true, schoolmaster?' Paulaine asked as if he hoped for an answer in the negative.

'I wanted her to be my wife,' the schoolmaster said.

'But she was already written for, Mr Schoolmaster.'

'I am very sorry.'

'So you make her with child, schoolmaster. You had interference with her?'

The schoolmaster bowed his head.

'You say it, schoolmaster. Say it with your mouth,' Paulaine cried.

'Yes,' the schoolmaster said in a very polite voice.

'I have to shoot you, Mr Schoolmaster,' Paulaine said very sadly.

'To shoot me will not bring back your daughter, Mr Dandrade.'

'I will have to shoot you, schoolmaster. A man lives in a certain way, by certain laws. I will have to shoot you.'

'It will not be wise. It will only add to your troubles, Mr Dandrade.'

'You have ruined my daughter. And now she is dead.'

'I have taught in your school, Mr Dandrade. I have made a village council in your village, and the road is now being built from Valencia.'

'There was crookedness in the road,' one of the Pampoon brothers said.

'I tried my best to give what I could, and I am very sorry for what has gone wrong. You must think now about your village, and about the school and the road.'

'I do not know how to think of anything, schoolmaster. I am dead inside of me. They will find someone to teach in the school. Why did you do this to make me have to shoot you, schoolmaster?'

'You do not have to shoot me. Here! This is all the money I have. I leave it with you, for the village.'

'And Christiana?'

'I am sorry about Christiana. I will go now.'

'You will go?'

Consantine Patron stood framed in the open doorway of the stable. Blood was running down the side of his head, and he held his shotgun in his hand.

'You will go?' he asked.

The schoolmaster put the small bag on the ground, and he took hold of the horse, and vaulted on to its bare back.

'I am riding now,' the schoolmaster said in a very polite and mild tone. 'I am very sorry.'

'I too am very sorry,' Paulaine said.

'Under different circumstances we would have said a much more affectionate goodbye.'

The schoolmaster was sitting very quietly on the back of the horse.

The sunshine was on the hills. The mist had disappeared. The villagers were looking at the face of Paulaine Dandrade.

Tears were in Paulaine's eyes.

'I have to shoot you, schoolmaster,' he said like a drugged man mumbling weakly and mechanically the last phrase suggested to him before his drugged state.

It was very quiet, and very cool, and the birds kept concerts in the grass, and trees, and the sleep had gone out of the people's faces.

'I am leaving all the money I own. I am riding on,' the schoolmaster said. 'I hope you get a better schoolteacher.'

Paulaine looked at the faces around him, helplessly.

'I have to shoot him,' he said weakly.

'It is not wise, Mr Dandrade. Truly.'

Paulaine looked at the shot-gun in his hand. He broke it. He put a cartridge into it. He kept looking at the shot-gun in his hands.

The schoolmaster said, 'Goodbye. I am going. Truly, it is not wise to shoot me now. I have done what I could. I have left everything I own.'

The horse started to walk. They watched it walk. The schoolmaster held himself erect on its back. The horse started to trot. They watched Paulaine. Then they turned again to the schoolmaster and the horse without saddle going at a nervous trot. Soon they would be out of range. The shot smashed the silence. The white horse seemed for a moment motionless in the air, then it pitched forward, fell, the schoolmaster going over its neck, with a swift, graceful pitch. The schoolmaster lay motionless.

The shot-gun in the hands of Consantine Patron was smoking still. Patron did not move, he broke the shot-gun, and took out the jacket of the shot, threw it into the bushes. Paulaine had a very stiff face on the verge of collapse.

'Mr Paulaine, why did you not shoot him?' Miguel the great one with the cocks asked.

Pauline did not answer. He went with the men who were walking to the place where the horse had fallen. The horse was stretched out, its mouth open, blood poured from a wound in the hip. It was twitching about, and was very pitiful to look at.

'The spine,' Francis Assivero said.

'Shoot it dead,' Paulaine said. 'Kill it.'

Assivero pressed his shot-gun against the chest of the horse, and shot it. It twitched, stretched out, and died.

The schoolmaster was lying motionless, with his hands stretched out in front him. His head was stuck into a stone, and there was blood.

Miguel, the great one with the cocks, said, 'This one is dead. The neck is broken.'

Constantine Patron looked at Paulaine.

'Why did you not shoot him, Paulaine?'

Pauline looked very beaten down and old.

'I do not know ... I love Kumaca ... I wanted this Kumaca to be

... to be ... I wanted Kumaca to have the progress like the other places. I fight for this school and this schoolmaster. I argue with you, Consantine, and I argue with the priest until we come to an understanding ... And my daughter is dead. Christiana is dead, and inside me, I am dead ... I do not know why I do not shoot him.'

Paulaine was crying.

Consantine Patron said, 'Come and go home. They will take up the body.'

'Yes, I better go home,' Paulaine said. 'Where is my daughter? ... I want to take her home. I will dig a grave and bury her. The priest is coming today. Will you come and help me with my daughter and the grave and the coffin to bury her? The priest is coming today.'

The dawn was gone now, and puffs of white clouds were drifting in the blue skies above Kumaca. Yellow butterflies hopped off leaves, went dodging in the sunshine, over shrubs and grass. Here and there a cock crowed, birds twittered, pecked ripe seeds off grass stems. The dew dried slowly, and doves walking on the ground drank water off the grass. In houses, the children were putting out the fathers' ancient suits in the sun, in preparation for the funeral when the priest came. It was very sad, and there would be no wake even.

Chapter Fourteen

I

The priest, Father Vincent, arrived to find Kumaca silent, two graves dug, and the villagers with closed, stony faces and suspicious eyes. A small group of men, which included Consantine Patron and Miguel, the great one with cocks, met him and took him around.

The schoolmaster is dead, they told him. He fell off his horse this morning and split his skull and broke his neck. They had dug a grave for him just in case. But perhaps the priest would like to take the body back to Zanilla where the schoolmaster perhaps had relatives who would themselves like to hold a funeral service for him?

Well, if the priest did not know of any relatives, they had better bury him right there in Kumaca. They had dug the grave for him, just in case. If it were all right, they would bury the body and the priest himself could say the mass.

Could he see the body?

Yes, the priest could see the body. But the horse was buried already. If he wanted to see the horse, they could dig it up for him.

No. He did not want to see the horse.

Very well. If he would follow them to the house where the schoolmaster had lived, they would show him the body.

There is the body.

The schoolmaster had been dressed in his black suit. The knot of his tie had been done a bit clumsy. Alive, the schoolmaster never would have worn it that way. It was obvious that he had no say in the matter. The eyes were quite closed. The lips were thick – perhaps a bit swollen, and rebellious-looking. Just a bit of the red on the inside showed. Without the spectacles, he had a weak-looking face – that is, except for the lips. His head was bandaged with a piece of white cotton, and the blood did not show.

Would the priest like to see the wound that split the skull?

No, no. He would not like to see it. But he would like to know how much it had cost to dig the grave and to prepare the coffin, and to do the various acts connected with the burial. All these were the responsibilities of the Church, since the schoolmaster also was the responsibility of the Church.

No. They did not want anything. They had done what had to be done. No, they did not want any payment. Was there anything else that the priest would like to know?

There was nothing else. He would bury the body right here in Kumaca. For one thing, it would not be easy to take it to Zanilla by donkey, over the rough road and the landslides; and where could he take it? He did not know of any relatives. The schoolmaster had lived very much to himself. He would bury the body right there. Of course, he would have to make a report to the police at Zanilla. That was the usual procedure in the case of accidents. But the police would take his word that everything was all right. However, one never knew, they might decide to investigate.

There is something more. The girl, Christiana, the daughter of Paulaine Dandrade . . . She also is dead. Drowned in the deep pool in the forest.

The girl?

Yes. The one only daughter of Paulaine is dead.

It is a great pity. She was a very pleasant child.

Yes, it is a great pity. And she was to be married to the son of Francis Assivero, the one called Pedro.

It is a great, a terrible tragedy for Kumaca.

It is indeed. Everybody is sad. She was a girl loved by all. And the family of Paulaine Dandrade is beside itself with grief. And the boy, the same Pedro to whom she was to be married, he was walking this morning all over the village, talking as if to the girl, as if Christiana were alive. It looked like he was going out of his head, and they had to hold him down. One of his friends hit him over the head with a piece of wood, and he went to sleep. It is very sad in the village today.

That is why the shop of Dardain is closed?

Dardain is very sad himself.

The family of Paulaine Dandrade must be very sad. He would go and extend his sympathy to them.

No, please. It would not be wise to do so at such a time. It was true that Paulaine was beside himself with grief. But he should be left alone. Perhaps another time when the priest comes to Kumaca.

Paulaine is the saddest of men today, and must be left alone with his grief.

All right. He would see Paulaine on another occasion. But they must tell Paulaine that the priest was very sympathetic.

Yes. That they will do.

Father Vincent did not ask many questions. When the time came, he said the mass over first one, then the other, dead body. He was numb inside, the priest was.

They laid Christiana in the little plot at the side of the house of Paulaine Dandrade, in which her mother had been buried. The schoolmaster was buried behind the school. There was a light drizzle when Christiana was being lowered into the grave, and the people stood there with the rain falling on them, and watched her being buried. The boy Pedro stood at the side of the grave, dressed in his best trousers and a black jacket which was obviously his father's. He looked at the coffin go down, then watched the diggers filling up the grave. He did not cry. His friends were very close around him, and when he took out his handkerchief, it was to wipe the rain off his face. He watched it all, and did not cry. The small brother of Christiana, the one called Humphy, was very brave also. He looked at the ceremony and did not cry. He broke away from his brothers and asked the priest was it true that Christiana would rise again. The priest told him yes, she would, and the small boy was very pleased, and did not shed a tear. Paulaine Dandrade was the only person that cried when the schoolmaster was being buried. He cried too much, and the villagers seemed a little ashamed of him. He cried much too much, and his eldest son Manuel, with his face very confused and knotted with sadness, held him up, otherwise he might have fallen. Paulaine Dandrade was very hard hit. It was all very sad, and the priest felt so numb and dry that he was not certain if all of it were true and not a dream.

It was a cool evening, and very silent. The priest did not linger after the funerals. Benn brought up the donkeys, and he and the acolytes mounted. He did not wave goodbye, even. It was not expected of him, either. They rode out of Kumaca in the thick, green, cool silence, and the priest did not look up to watch the parrots crossing, squawking in the sky over his head. It was very green, the country. That was because of the high forest and the hills, and the rainfall these attracted. Perhaps when the road came in from Valencia, forestry would become an industry. They would cut out much of the valuable timber. Tractors would come up, and men with axes and canthooks and saws, and trucks with winches would come up to reel up the logs and transport them. Then there would not be so much greenness, and not so much rain, and the parrots would cross in another sky.

Silence now. Butterflies dodging in the sunshine over shrubs, trees murmuring with wind; and the king-of-the-woods at the edge of the forest, making its doleful call. Silence. Humming-birds hovering over petals of red hibiscus flowers spotting the track's edge; and the sound of water running over stones down in the valley where balisier flowers stood innocent of their beauty, the way some village girls are until the strangers come in, until the sweet mouths of strangers turn them to lipsticks and mirrors. Silence, and the many fingers of para grass at the roadside, pointing to the earth from which their roots sprang, gesturing skyward when the wind commanded.

Silence for Benn to break.

'You think they kill him, priest?'

'He is dead.'

'Yes, he is dead.'

Silence. The plopping of the donkey's faeces on the track, the bugle-note crack of one donkey passing wind, another donkey whipping flies off its rump.

'I never like him. I do not say he was not good. I say only that for myself I never like the man.'

The priest did not say anything.

'I know it is not good to talk bad of the dead, but I say just how I feel. His way was too much like the way of Captain Grant who shoot my horse . . . Priest, maybe he was a good man. He look too big in acting. I suspect a man who look too big in acting. I think that inside such a man, he is not big.'

'He is dead,' the priest said. 'I think perhaps he tried his best.'

'Priest, some men do not know what their best is. They do not do things from inside of them. They do not know how it is inside their own hearts.'

'It is not easy to know yourself. Only after a long time, and with much suffering . . . after a long time . . . after many dyings . . .'

Birds flapping wings. One acolyte coughing nervously.

'You talk with much sadness, priest, as if you had many dyings,' Benn said.

'One grows old . . . one dies again and again.'

'And this thing with the schoolmaster?'

'It was not pleasant. I remember all the time how eager Paulaine Dandrade looked when he came to see me that morning. It is very hard with him now.'

'Yes, he was crying. It really was hard with him. But Consantine Patron was himself. Like myself, he did not much like the schoolmaster.'

'Patron was the one who could have been of great assistance, but he chose to stand by and look on.'

'Then it is too late, eh . . . Hmm! Hmm!' Benn said.

Silence as the party dismounted to cross the landslide, carefully, efficiently. And now they were mounted again.

'You will have to get another schoolmaster, priest.'

'Yes, the school is there.'

'You cannot close it down.'

'It is how things are. Something begins, it continues.'

'Maybe next time . . . sometime . . . you get someone from the village to teach school,' Benn said, then he added: 'Or maybe with the road opened the teacher if he from outside can travel to and from Kumaca.'

'The opening of the road will bring its own difficulties,' the priest said.

Silence. Wind, and tree leaves waving like flags.

'Do you have a cigarette, priest?'

'Here is one.'

'Thank you. I have matches.'

The scratch of the match now. Benn bends his head to the flame, puffs once on the cigarette, puffs again.

'You think of the road, priest. There is no need to be sad because of the road. It had to happen. Sometime it would have to be open.'

'I had a hope for Kumaca. Paulaine Dandrade when he came to see me about the school did not understand what I was trying to say. He did not know that I was not against him.'

'Your face is white, priest. Perhaps he does not trust that.'

'And my gown is white. I chose my gown, I did not choose my face.'

'Your intentions are good, priest. All of us have good intentions, eh. I say I would give my horse to that man. He shoot the horse, priest. He shoot my horse. That is the world, eh. And when the man shoot my horse, priest, it hurt, and I wanted to kill the man. I want to live, priest, and if I shoot the man, priest, the police . . . The police . . . The hangman . . . And I want to live. To live, a man has to find a way.'

'Have you found that way?'

'I try, priest. Try. And soon I see I will have again to learn how to live. They are building this road and will not need my donkeys any more.'

'What will you do?'

'I do not know exactly. I think to take my family to Kumaca and there make a garden and plant yams and sell. And I think to take them to Zanilla where the living is faster than they know. I think of my children, priest. My wife is not young anymore, but she is a good woman and I think of her. But my children, priest. All the time I think of my children. The land in Kumaca is rich and would bring good yams, and there is a school now, but . . . I will talk to my wife about it. One of these days, if you have a mind to, you must come and see my wife and the children we have, priest. It is a small place we live in, but my wife will get fussy and make a big welcome for you, and I also will be happy.'

'It will be a great honour for me,' Father Vincent said. 'But I would not like Mrs Benn to put herself out too much for me.'

'You cannot stop that, priest. If she does not make a fuss all the beauty and appreciation goes from your visit. For a woman, to make a fuss is a great and wonderful thing.'

Father Vincent smiled.

'I will be happy to come. I shall tell you the day.'

Dusk was falling now and birds were flying low to their nests. The priest did not speak and drifted into silence and his aloneness. Benn's donkey moved once more to the head of the party. They came around a bend in the road and saw Valencia with the lights going on in the houses. The acolytes became very gay and started to talk very much, and the donkey that had made the most runs between Kumaca and Valencia began to bray and broke into a trot and surprised the acolyte on its back who was completing his first trip.

Also by Earl Lovelace

The Dragon Can't Dance

Trinidad, 1970s. Calvary Hill – poverty-stricken and rubbish-strewn – is home to a community of people who come together during the joyful yearly town Carnival, becoming larger-than-life versions of themselves. But when it ends, and the strains of day-to-day life grow large, what happens to the people's hopes, and the feeling that 'all o' we is one'?

With an unforgettable cast of characters, *The Dragon Can't Dance* is a powerful novel about the desire for identity and belonging, alongside the legacies of a colonial past.

'A landmark, not in the West Indian, but in the contemporary novel.' C. L. R. James

'Trinidad . . . is evoked in generous, torrential prose that seems to hold every complexity – of history, of ethnicity, of reason and magic alike – within its rushing energy.' *New York Times*

'Earl Lovelace's writing has a picturesque yet dark energy, with a carnival snaking through the novel like a dangerous spine.' *Guardian*

faber

Also by Earl Lovelace

Salt

Alford, the youngest son of a poor farm worker in Trinidad, has risen above his class to become a respected schoolteacher. Idealistic and determined, he journeys to the capital city to campaign for his community and quickly becomes a local hero. It truly seems that anything is possible . . .

Salt tells the story of a country through an unforgettable cast of characters, who with wit and passion are striving to tell their stories and make sense of life in an evolving homeland.

'An amazingly vivid and joyous novel . . . a carnival of creole sounds.' *The Times*

'Superb . . . A moving sense of history.' *Mail on Sunday*

'A novel confident in its rhythms, in the authority of its selling, driven by exultant compassion for its characters.' Derek Walcott

faber

Also by Earl Lovelace

Is Just a Movie

Winner of the OCM Bocas Prize for Caribbean Literature

In Trinidad, in the wake of the 1970 Black Power rebellion, we follow Sonnyboy, singer KingKala, and their town's folk through experiments in music, politics, religion, love, and their day-to-day adventures. When a film crew arrives on the island to shoot a movie, they hope it will help make their name – but nothing turns out as they expect. Humorous and serious, sad and uplifting, *Is Just a Movie* is a radiant novel about small moments of magic in ordinary life.

'Funny, moving and endlessly inventive.' *The Times*

'A master storyteller.' *Financial Times*

'Lovelace is bursting with things to say about this complex, heterogeneous society in the late twentieth century. This he does with a flair that at its best reaches a soaring rhapsody. The scabs of racial tension are cautiously peeled back and we witness the community's loves, aspirations and machinations; their little victories and defeats, their best selves and worst selves.' Bernardine Evaristo, *Guardian*

faber